A WOMAN IN THE HOUSE

A Woman in the House

William E. Barrett

Doubleday & Company, Inc.
Garden City, New York

For
Grace and Cullen
and
Evelyn and Howard

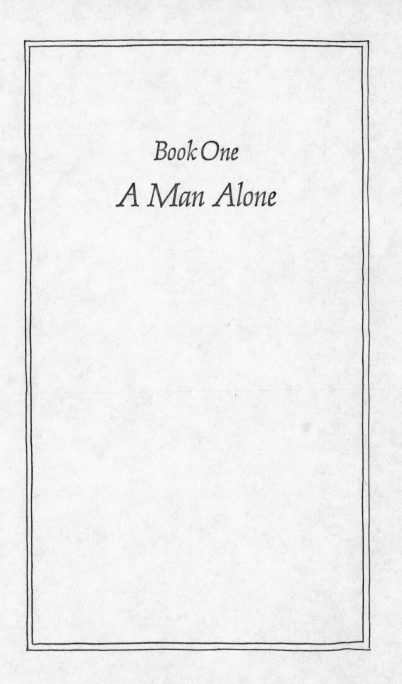

Book One

A Man Alone

Chapter One

His name was Konrad, or he assumed that it was. There was another name, a family name, on his identification papers but he had never believed in it. He had no sense of family, of being related to anybody or to anything. As far as his memory could tell him anything about himself, he had been born in a monastery with no woman present, no woman concerned with him. He was a Monk and had always been a Monk, but he was not a priest and he had no feeling of commitment to an organized religion; all of which made sense to him, beyond any need for worry or for pondering the reasons behind the existence of things.

He was twenty-four years old on a spring day, a stateless person who had been born, if born any place, in Russia. His early memories were Russian memories and his first language, although he grew up speaking several other languages as well, was Russian. He walked a forest road in Germany and he had walked that road for many miles over many days. He had a two-wheeled cart with a long shank, designed originally for people who traveled in small boats on fast rivers. There were always stretches of rushing water too furious for small boats to navigate and the little cart, unfolded, would carry the boat over the portage.

Konrad, who had never owned a boat, had purchased his cart, secondhand, in a small town beside an Austrian river. He carried all of his possessions in it, carefully rolled and tied and packed. It was the solitary companion of his journeying. He sometimes pulled it but normally he pushed.

The day had been warm and it did not cool with the gathering of the shadows. Konrad's muscles were insisting that he had reached the end of day and he was in a mood to listen to them when he heard the voices. They were young voices. He heard then a thudding sound and the sharp crackle of breaking glass.

There was a clearing in the forest, a man-made clearing, oval in shape with an oblong, single-story wooden house at the north end of the oval, carefully and skillfully constructed of nailed planks but never painted. It was the kind of house constructed by armies, needed for some temporary purpose but not designed for a long life. There were four boys at the south end of the oval. They had been throwing rocks at the house but they stopped when they saw Konrad, a study in suspended action, holding their missiles. Konrad walked into the clearing, placing himself between the boys and the house. One of the boys, the tallest of the four, immediately threw his rock. It missed Konrad by less than six inches and thudded against the plank wall. He stood facing the youth, aware that the throwing of the rock was a challenge, aware, too, that the other boys had spread out, moving in toward him, a human arc which confronted him with two ends and a middle. They were boys of sixteen or seventeen; sturdy, combative, preferring perhaps combat with a man to the bombardment of a house. Konrad concentrated his attention on the obvious leader, the boy who had thrown the rock at him.

"It is very easy to destroy things," he said. "Why do you do easy things?"

The boy frowned. He was shaggy-haired and his clothes were shabby. There was hostility in his eyes, in his face, in the lines of his body.

"What do you care?" he said.

"I would like to live in that house."

"You can't. It was a whorehouse. We are going to knock it down."

Konrad shrugged. He doubted that these four young men would undertake the labor of destroying a solid house. They would satisfy themselves by mutilating it. He detested that. He hated vandalism worse than he hated theft, hated the breaking of anything which the breaker was incapable of replacing. It was one of the few hatreds that moved in him and he was capable of controlling it. He turned his back to the youths and took two steps toward the house. The leader moved, coming in on his left, dropping his hand to grip the handle of the cart. Konrad stiffened.

"Take your hand off my cart," he said.

The boy ignored him, tightening his grip, thrusting his shoulder against Konrad's. There was strength in him. Konrad's hand dropped to the hand on the cart handle, dropped and tightened, twisting slightly. He read surprise in the boy's eyes before he read hurt there. He held his grip when the other's hand left the cart handle. He had strong hands, incredibly strong hands, and he understood the laws of leverage.

The boy tried to turn, tried to strike with his free hand, but he was up on his toes, off balance and unable to anchor his weight. His face was pale but he tightened his lips against each other.

The boys had drawn closer. Konrad was aware of them

but there was a reality in this situation which excluded them. The boy whose hand he crushed could call for help and have it immediately. That would change the reality. The three boys would attack, or they would let the one boy fight his own battle. It depended upon what the boy wanted. The boy knew that as Konrad knew it. There was a blue line in the corner of his mouth and agony in his eyes but he did not ask for help and he did not ask for release. Konrad relaxed his grip suddenly and stepped back.

"You are, perhaps, a good man," he said. "I could like you."

"I do not want you to like me. When my hand feels better I will fight you."

"To gain what?"

Konrad stood quietly, asking the question with his eyes as well as with his voice. When the boy did not answer he turned away, pushing the cart close to the house, loosening the canvas cover. He could feel the boys behind him, chained momentarily by indecision but capable of swift action. A heavy voice said:

"We should kick him around, Werner. We should kick him around."

"No. He's mine. I'll take care of him."

Konrad recognized the voice of the boy who had tried to seize his cart. It was interesting that his name was Werner. One could remember a human being without remembering a name, as one remembered a nameless tree or a nameless bird, but there was interest in the idea that this boy was called Werner. Konrad took his flashlight from his cart. He could examine the exterior of this building in the fading daylight but he would need a light for exploration indoors. It would be possible to spend the night here, perhaps many nights.

He heard the boys moving away. There was menace in their silent withdrawal. They would return, certainly. Werner had pledged himself to revenge and the others seemed to welcome the idea of violence for its own sake. They could determine the time of their return, day or night, and Konrad would not know what they had decided until they came. He shrugged.

There were stenciled initials on the side of the house: *U.S.A.* For whatever use they had for it, this had belonged to the United States Army. There were American soldiers still in Germany, most of them men who had been born after the war between the two nations was over. The Americans were no longer in the Munich area and this spot in which he found himself was on the edge or the outskirts of Munich. He was still surrounded by the atmosphere of trees and running water but there was something in the air that a man's nerves could feel, the nearness of a city, of packed and crowded life, a vibration perhaps from traffic in the near distance.

He pushed the door of the house open, aware that there had been a padlock securing it which someone had removed. To his surprise the beam of his flashlight moved over a reasonably clean floor. There was no debris, no clutter. He was in a fairly large room, approximately 16′ by 12′. There was only one window, the one broken by the boys. The walls were white. At the far end of the room there was a pattern of holes drilled into the floor.

"Some kind of a machine," he said.

Armies did many mysterious things. This might have been a radio check point of some kind, or a place for processing photographs or a small printing plant, a place for duplicating documents. There was little point in guessing, particularly since the guesser had never been in an army. He moved on to the next room. There was a short hall with small rooms on either side, a medium-sized room at the end. There had been electricity. Light sockets remained in the ceilings, without bulbs. There were switches in the walls, the remains of obvious telephone connections in the baseboard. Beyond the last room there was a toilet and, to Konrad's surprise, it flushed when he pressed the control knob. There was a washbasin but no bath, no shower. Obviously men had worked here but had not lived here.

He walked back, examining the rooms more carefully. When he flashed his light into one of the small side rooms, he discovered lettering on the white wall: bold, firm black letters which spelled HAARIGE MARIE. He remembered the boys saying that this had been a whorehouse. That name on the wall was the only detail that would suggest any such use for the place: HAIRY MARY.

He wondered about that. He had never had anything to do with whores or whorehouses but he knew about them. He had lived in Vienna, in one of the very poor sections of Vienna.

The heavy dusk had moved into the clearing and the trees at the far end were a dark mass without detail. Konrad took a tin box from his pack. He had cheese in that and two rolls and an apple. When he could not obtain, or prepare, a hot meal a supper such as this was enough. He ate slowly, looking into the thickening shadows. He was very fortunate, he thought, very fortunate indeed, to find such a place as this, even if he did not keep it for long. He was in Munich and he had a place in which to live.

Chapter Two

Konrad had learned prayer at the monastery, the formal prayers and those devotions which only a Monk would call prayer. He started his day, always, with the formal prayers, words that someone else had strung together and which he had merely memorized; the ending of his day was his own. He prayed then by sitting motionless and permitting his day, or some portion of his life, to unreel in his mind, not planning the unreeling nor setting the sequences, merely waiting quietly for thought to come to him. He offered his thought and the deeds of his life to God, neither justifying them nor seeking judgment on them. He had learned that form of prayer when he was very young.

"Lift your thought to God," Father Stephen told him. "You do not need words."

With the maturing years he doubted that the Creator of the universe had time for so humble a creature as himself, but he did not doubt the reality of prayer. Never. Someone shared his prayer, particularly the evening prayer, someone invisible, someone close to him. He felt the other presence and respected it, not presuming to believe that it was God, but content that it was of God, or sent by God, a creature of God's purpose. He did not ponder beyond that point. It was not a necessity of his faith that he be supplied with the answers to riddles, or with keys for the unlocking of mysteries. His own life was sufficiently strange to baffle him; he did not have to reach out beyond the universe.

The dark had dropped down into the clearing and there was a new moon visible above the tops of the trees. Stars were scattered across the sky and Konrad could hear three separate choirs of insects. He sat on the ground before the wooden structure which American soldiers had built and in which, seemingly, someone named Hairy Mary had lived. His body was relaxed, his legs folded under him in the Buddha position. He faced the far end of the clearing where there was no light, real or reflected.

There had been boys in this clearing who had nothing to do but wander in the woods and throw rocks at an empty building. One did not pass judgments. The woods were there. He had walked in them all this day, and in other days. The rocks were there. Boys, perhaps, could have an irresistible urge to throw rocks at something. Konrad did not know. He had never been a boy; he had always been a Monk. How old were these boys? Sixteen or seventeen? No more than that. It was not so very long since he had been sixteen or seventeen but he did not know, at this moment, what he had been doing then, or thinking. He made no attempt to know. In his hour of prayer he offered his mind to God and let thought flow into it without attempting to direct the flow. It was not easy to step aside from oneself in that manner; it took years to learn how it was done. A Monk, perhaps, was alone in being able to sit quietly on the surface of his life, permitting thought, or memory, to rise unsummoned from the depths of his own being.

Nothing had ever come up to Konrad which belonged

to time before the monastery, nothing but one vivid moment. On all of the evidence of his own knowing, he had been born in the monastery but he had seen his father shot. He could not remember one feature of the man's face nor whether he was short or tall. He could not remember a word nor the touch of a hand, nothing that would identify the man in any relationship to himself; but he had known that the man who was shot had been his father. He had been standing beside the man, looking up at him, when the sharp banging sound of the fired gun shook the room. He remembered the sound as he remembered the blood flowing out of his father's face, and his father falling forward. He remembered a voice screaming and soldiers taking a woman out of the room, taking her away forcibly, roughly. He did not remember one feature of the woman's face nor what she wore, but he knew that she was his mother.

The film that ran in his mind was cut there. He could not remember himself in the scene. He did not know if he had cried or if he had attempted to run, whether he was frightened or whether any one spoke to him. He could not remember the soldiers nor what kind of uniforms they wore, nor remember how he knew that they were soldiers. All of his boyhood and his babyhood was in that one remembered moment of time. There was nothing before it, nothing at all; after it, he was a Monk.

Father Stephen told him one day, when he was old enough to be told of serious matters, that a woman of the village had picked him up in her arms and carried him to the priest. Father Stephen was a catacomb priest then, a Russian Orthodox priest who had refused allegiance to the State-controlled Hierarchy. Father Stephen worked in the underground and he was in danger from the soldiery himself but he had accepted the small boy from the woman.

Konrad did not remember the woman, not even with a flash of memory. He did not know the name of the town. The soldiers, whom he did not remember, were unquestionably Russian because the town, whatever its name, was in Russia and the year was 1949. The first memory that Konrad had, the first memory linked to later events, was of looking up into brown eyes in a bearded face.

"Do not be afraid," a soft voice said. "No one will hurt you."

His life, as far as Konrad was concerned, began then. He was not quite five so the early pattern was blurred but he traveled in the night with the big bearded man and they slept in the daylight hours, hidden away often in barns and cellars. Somewhere on the journey he learned that the man was called Father Stephen, but he could never remember later how he learned that, or when. They came at last to the monastery which was to be Konrad's world for ten years.

The monastery stood on a hill which rose above a wide river; a series of onion-shaped towers and stone walls and intricately wrought gates. Inside there were long corridors with dark gray walls and uneven stone flooring, huge work rooms, chapels rich in ikons and frescoes. A Monk slept on a hard narrow bed, wrapped in his blankets. Some of the Monks were careless about bathing but, from the beginning, Father Stephen insisted that the boy must be clean, that he must bathe regularly as he did himself. Konrad accepted what he was told to do. There were no alternatives offered to him. The rules of the monastery and its customs were the norm of living. There was nothing else.

He asked Father Stephen one day about his mother. "What happened to her?" he said.

Father Stephen did not look at him. He raised his head as he did in some of the most solemn moments of prayer.

"They killed her, too," he said.

"But wasn't there any one else? I don't know who I am. I can't remember."

Father Stephen looked at him then. "You know as much about yourself as you were meant to know," he said. "Be content. If God wanted you to remember you would remember."

"You have a past. I've heard you talk of Kiev where you were born. Other Monks have pasts and they remember them. I would like to know about myself."

Father Stephen was a man of magnificent appearance. He had a short dark beard and curling hair and bronzed skin. His face was broad and his eyes dark brown. He had large, white even teeth. There was kindness in him, gentleness, and he never evaded questions or refused to answer questions; but, somehow, his answers were often inadequate.

"Your origin makes no difference," he said. "You are here. You owe the past for nothing except your life and you will pay that debt ultimately by dying."

In the monastery some knowledge had to be absorbed rather than learned. Some things were so obvious, rooted in the fact of being a Russian, that it was impossible to explain them. There were no boys in the monastery except Konrad. He had no contact with children. A Soviet law explained that. No one under eighteen was permitted to join a church. Konrad's presence was a great secret in which, ultimately, the Monks took delight, even those who were known as "Soviet Monks" because their first loyalty was to the State rather than to the church. There were both Soviet Monks and Catacomb Monks in the same monastery, aware of one another as opposing forces but living together in comparative harmony because they were artists. The monastery had recruited its Monks from all over Russia and from some of the satellites, men with strange skills. The government sent to them tons of damaged art objects, relics of the war. The Monks as restorers achieved near-miracles.

Konrad took the near-miracles for granted in the process of growing up. They were the commonplaces of his life. He learned patience as the silent assistant of patient men and he acquired skills of his own without being aware that he was acquiring them. He shared in a great sense of excitement as beauty emerged from what had been wreckage. He was never to forget that, the joy of bringing beauty into the world, of seeing it emerge, of feeling a part of it.

Conspiracy was part of his growing, too, the knowledge that a brutal, aggressive force existed, that one should avoid being crushed by it and one should be careful that no act of carelessness betrayed another to destruction.

"Never remember the name of a place or of a person," Father Stephen told him. "Cast names out of your mind."

Konrad tried to obey that injunction but he did not understand it in his early years. Places and persons, it seemed, should not have names if one were forbidden to remember them. Ultimately, he lived in a world in which names had little significance. He could not name the trees or the birds, the flowers or the small animals; if ever he learned the names, he blocked them out. Towns were merely towns and people, people. He accompanied Father Stephen, as he grew older, on trips to loyal Christians of the old order. He gloried in the solemn Masses in cellars and hidden places, proud of his role as altar boy, but he did not know where the cellars and the hidden places were.

Father Stephen was the compelling figure in his life,

one of the few who moved in his mind with a name. There were intervals of time when he did not see him but he never had the sense that Father Stephen was far away. He believed as a boy, and still believed, that Father Stephen was the most magnificent of men; in appearance, in voice, in manner, in his gift of command, in the fervor of his prayer.

Father Stephen was not quite six feet tall. He was in his fifties during the time that Konrad remembered best. He looked at one intently but there was understanding in his eyes. He had a deep laugh when he laughed. He was a saintly man with a deep love of God in his soul, and a great patience with man, but he was not a Saint. He enjoyed drinking beer or wine in villages where he had close friends and sometimes, not often, he drank too much. He sang the folk songs and the songs of toil and the comical ballads with the same authority that he brought to Masses. He laughed heartily when the party pleased him and he refused to quarrel with the occasional quarrelsome man.

"You cannot know what devils in a man's life are beating him," he would tell Konrad. "Do not, in your pride, believe that you have created his anger. That anger is his own and it may be that he knows from whence it comes."

He was a great traveling companion, Father Stephen. He knew legends and stories and stirring romantic tales. He knew the histories of points with strange names, the points of obscurity. He was a Ukrainian, proud of his birth in the holy city of Kiev. He knew marvelous stories of Kiev in the days of its glory. "It had over four hundred churches at one time in the city," he said, "but the man who wrote of that was a great liar so the figure is probably an exaggeration."

Travel, even when one saw only villages at night, was exciting but the monastery was the great reality. Konrad studied languages under patient men who taught him as a service to God. He learned many languages and he learned them well. He studied the Bible and the history of the Orthodox faith, but he learned no general history, ancient or modern, into which he could fit the Church. He learned in outline the geography of Russia and of the countries which touched it, but he had a confused picture of the world. He could not imagine an ocean.

It was astonishing what a boy could learn when there were no distractions, when learning was the aim. Konrad learned to play the piano reasonably well, and the organ; ultimately how to tune a piano. He learned to sketch, to paint in oils, to carve wood. He was fascinated by the objects damaged in the war and, at a late date, being restored: paintings, sculpture, ikons, bronzes, tapestries, carved pieces, candelabra, very old furnishings. The government tolerated this aggregation of odd Monks, many of whom were too religious to be tolerated happily, because only in a monastery could intricately lovely things be brought back to beauty. The Monks, if they did not have the required skills, were expected to develop them. Konrad was a Monk.

It was a large monastery, a series of buildings rather than one building. A person had his quota of exercise each day if he kept schedules of work and study in many places, as Konrad did; but his pattern of living included exercises.

A monastery, an old monastery, needed constant care, repairs and repainting. The younger men were expected to climb ladders and haul loads, to do ordinary carpentry work and to be electricians or stone masons or painters. A man walked and stretched and lifted and climbed, keeping health in his muscles. A man did not know what laziness was because no one in the man's world was lazy. Conditions did not permit letdown.

Sex education, as far as Konrad was concerned, had been a simple matter. Father Stephen had permitted him to watch the mating of animals, making no point of it. Ultimately the priest told him that human beings obeyed the same laws of nature, that children grew out of the mating.

"It is for people who are married," he said simply. "It is not for Monks. A Monk gives himself to God."

The matter of sex never came up again in his relationship with Stephen who, as a priest, talked of sin as sin, seldom finding it necessary to be specific. In Vienna, on his own, Konrad had discovered that sex was not as simple as Father Stephen pictured it, but he was still not certain that he would have been better served if he had been more fully educated. One found his way in that as in most things.

Ten years in a monastery had taught him many things, prepared him for many things. He could not criticize it for ignoring facets of life that were non-monastery. He came a long way from the monastery in Vienna but, in a sense, he had carried the monastery with him. Sitting in the darkness on the outskirts of Munich, he faced another of the many things that he had not been taught.

He did not understand the boys of the afternoon. He might possibly have turned out as they did if he had lived in their environment. He had known no other boys in his growing up so he had no idea of what it might be like to travel in a group as these boys did. He did not feel opposed to them. They did not stand between him and anything that he wanted, nor did he provide any obstacles to them; yet they felt hostility toward him and he lacked the wisdom to deal with that hostility, to brush it out of their lives and out of his. He believed as Father Stephen believed—"A person who comes into your life is an opportunity of your soul"—but he did not know what, precisely, he would do when the boys came back, as they certainly would come back.

He rose and stood for a minute, looking at the starry sky, then went inside. He rolled himself in two blankets and he was asleep in five minutes.

Chapter Three

The structure in which he had spent the night did not look as fresh to Konrad in the morning. The walls were streaked and stained and the floors in the two small rooms decidedly dirty. Everything that had been built into the structure had been removed. He could see where the wires had been and the bolts which held equipment in place. He doubted that the electrical system remaining in the building was connected. He could not test it without a light bulb. There was a washbasin in the rear room and the water ran, a toilet in a small room with a flusher that flushed.

There was a message written on the white wall of the toilet room. Someone had lettered in a firm black script: *Do not wear a hat while sitting on the can.*

Konrad read the message, and reread it. English was one of the languages he had studied in the monastery and he had had practice in it during his time in Vienna. Many people in Vienna spoke English, or tried to speak it. He had read newspapers printed in English with little difficulty. He read the message for the third time.

Do not wear a hat while sitting on the can.

It made no sense to him. He dismissed it. There were matters of greater importance. He was astonished that he had running water and he was grateful for it. There were scars on the baseboards where, he judged, electric heating panels had been. The Americans had probably taken the heating system when they left.

Out of doors, the early morning was bright and clear. The trees, being German trees, stood straight in precise rows with no underbrush beneath them. He could hear the singing sound of the stream that he had followed yesterday. It was beyond the trees where he could not see it. His supplies were low. He had only two slices of stale bread for breakfast. He sat on the ground to eat them. His prayers, the formal prayers of his day, had been said when he first awakened but he made the Sign of the Cross over his breakfast as Father Stephen had made the Sign over every meal.

Birds of various sizes and colors dropped into the clearing as soon as he started to eat. They watched him expectantly and he stared stoically back. He was never sentimental about birds and he was certain that birds were not sentimental about him. He did not give them any of his breakfast.

Exploring his new environment would have been simpler without his two-wheeled cart and he weighed the idea of leaving it in the structure. There was a closet in the back room which would hold it and it would probably be safe, but all that he owned was under the canvas of that two wheeler which had been designed to carry a *Faltboot*, one of those little boats in which men challenged the fast, narrow rivers. He could not afford to lose what it carried so he took the cart with him.

He wore his black Monk's robe, a cassock-like garment. It was comfortable and he was at home in it and it gained him an acceptance which he would not have without it. Bavaria, like Austria, was largely Roman Catholic and accustomed to priests, friars, and Monks of various orders. Konrad always identified himself as a Russian Orthodox Monk when he had the opportunity and he never claimed to be a priest or a Roman Catholic but people accepted him for what he suggested to them. He never imposed on them and he never begged but the acceptance of people often provided him with work to do. Some of his happiest adventures had come to him when priests hired him to clean and repair the treasures in their churches, but most priests were cold to him. He could understand that. Father Stephen had never warmed to Catholics or to Protestants, either.

There was a sign that read *Zeitplatz Ganzjährie* (camping site all the year) less than half a mile from the structure in which he had spent the night. A man and a woman and two children were having breakfast at one of the tables. There was no one else in the park. Here was a place where a man could cook his food. There was a shelter house and a number of tables. Konrad had found many of these along the route that he had followed through Germany. In the summer, he was certain, this one, so close to Munich, would be crowded but that did not matter.

He walked to the main highway which carried the traffic to and from the autobahn. There was something else that he had to find and he found it on the edge of a suburban village: a white, rectangular building with a sign which read, BAD.

This was the bathhouse. Many of these settlements of small houses had toilets indoors but no baths. The bathhouse served the community. For one mark a man could have a shower, for two marks a tub bath. Some bathhouses had swimming pools. A man such as himself, with a solid shelter, a year-round camping ground and a bathhouse, all within easy walking distance of each other, was a man who had everything.

Konrad purchased a small order of groceries at a store south of the village, then walked back to his clearing. Three of yesterday's four boys were sitting in the shade on the clearing's edge. They were smoking oddly shaped cigarettes and it was obvious that they had been awaiting Konrad's return. His robe disconcerted them. He noted that as he noted the fact that yesterday's leader, the boy whose hand he had gripped, was missing. He entered his house, put his groceries in the back room and took a hammer, nails, and a saw from his pack. There were shelves in the closet and he removed two of them. He would buy glass for the broken window if he discovered that he could stay in the wooden structure but, in the meantime, the window had to be boarded up. He removed his robe and hung it in the closet.

The boys rose and crossed the clearing when he came out. They had a different leader today, a short, stocky youth with straight black hair which came down over his forehead to his eyebrows. One of the boys behind him was tall and thin, the other, medium tall, wore glasses.

"We did not know that you were a priest," the leader said. His voice was hostile.

"I am not. I'm a Monk, a Russian Orthodox Monk."

"A Russian!" The tall, thin boy spat. "All Russians are sons of bitches."

Konrad looked at him. "Russians, all Russians, are sons of men," he said, "or daughters of men, as Germans are."

"Russians are sons of bitches," the tall boy repeated. It seemed to be the sum total of all that he had to say because he stood silent after he said it. The leader thrust his chin forward.

"We do not want you here," he said.

"Are your wants of any importance?"

"You're damned right. We can make you leave."

Konrad shrugged. "I don't know why you should," he said.

He measured the window, paying no further attention to the boys. The leader yesterday had had fire and aggressiveness in him. If he were here these youths would be dangerous but without him they lacked initiative. One of them threw a small stone which bounced off a board, a foot from Konrad's head. He did not look around. The two boards would cover the window and there was no necessity for sawing them. Konrad held the first in place and drove his nails. The three youths sat on the ground and indulged in rapid-fire comment on him and on the work that he was doing. They were good at this. They used dirty language but some of their comments were funny. They flipped pebbles at him, or small stones, sometimes hitting him, sometimes not. He finished nailing the second board and turned around.

He stood then, looking at them and they stared at him vacantly. They seemed to have dissipated their hostility in talk and in the tossing of small stones. He turned away from them, picked up his tools and went into the house.

He knew then, with fair certainty, what was the matter with them. The odd-shaped cigarettes they had been smoking were probably marijuana. Some of the young people of Vienna smoked it while he lived there. It came from Africa through Italy to Austria. The regular smokers lacked drive and initiative, making a virtue of their withdrawal from all activity. They used the drug as a tranquilizer. When they smoked, nothing seemed to matter; problems were non-existent, trouble faded away. "I like it that way," a smoker told him once.

Konrad fixed his lunch. He did not know that these

young people smoked marijuana, he told himself; he merely suspected it. It was an expensive habit in Vienna and it would probably be expensive here. He knew nothing about these youths, where or how they obtained money, whether they took other drugs, or took drugs at all. They were hostile toward him with no reason for the hostility, unless the fact of his being a stranger and a Russian could be a reason. Without the dulling of a tranquilizer that hostility might have come to focus today. It might come to focus, tranquilizer or no tranquilizer, when yesterday's leader returned from wherever he had gone.

Konrad sat on the floor in the largest room and ate his lunch. There was nothing that he could do about trouble while it was still down the road. He would, he decided, go to the camping grounds tonight and cook a hot meal.

When he went out again to the clearing the boys had gone.

Chapter Four

It was time to earn a living in Germany. Konrad had very little money and he had not worked in weeks. He had entered Germany, necessarily, as a Stateless person and qualifying for admittance had been rather slow work. The men who ran the grim, cheerless bureau at Zirndorf, the admittance point, were efficient and coolly detached, caring less for people, perhaps, than for the procedures which governed the qualifying or disqualifying of people. Konrad had been one of the fortunate knockers at the gate. Some people with complicated histories and no passports had been forced to spend weeks in Zirndorf.

Konrad had not sought work to do short of Munich. It was the destination that he had set for himself and he had pursued a zigzag route, seeing the country, learning to feel at home in it.

He had many skills that he had learned in the monastery. He could clean, repair, and restore precious things, or quite ordinary things which the possessors considered precious. He had patience and sure hands and the knowledge of materials. He could make broken jewelry whole again or bring a dull, dim painting to life. He liked to work with religious articles: ikons, which would be rare in this country, or statues, images, preferably wood carvings; or chalices and candlesticks. The war had marred so many things and for years no one could afford to have anything fixed. It was different now but most people were still careful. He had learned that in Austria but people needed the skills that he had and he charged little. He worked for the work's sake, not for money.

A museum would be the ideal place for him to work but in Austria the professionals in the museums had not liked his monastic background. He was not one of their guild, nor one of their kind. He had worked for a dealer in antiques who had valued him but he could take no joy out of restoring beauty when the purpose of the restoration was the making of profit for a proprietor. He had taken joy out of walking the roads and the streets, ringing bells or knocking on doors. People in humble houses owned astonishing things and so many of the things they owned were damaged in one way or another.

He would walk the streets of Munich and he would, he was certain, find work to do. If he could not gain admittance to a house in any other way, he could offer to tune the piano. That was a long, patient task but worth effort. So many of the Austrian homes, even poor ones, had housed pianos and Germany loved music as Austria did. The people who had challenging work for him to do were, with few exceptions, people who had little money. He was poorly paid but he shared the food of many families and he had a rich satisfaction in the small miracles which happened under his fingers. He was happy that he was a Monk, needing little. There were few men as free as he.

He was sorting and arranging his stock of oils and chemicals and stains and glues when the police came. They drove to the edge of the clearing in a black Volkswagen. They were tall men, one of them middle-aged and the

other man young. Their uniforms had seen fairly long
wear. It was the usual thing, Konrad had noted, for police
in Germany to look like hard-working citizens rather
than like gleaming military, disclaiming in their appearance
any association with a Police State. The middle-aged of-
ficer was coldly polite.

"May I see your papers?" he said.

"I'll get them."

Konrad regretted that he was not wearing his black
Monk's robe for this interview but it was, perhaps, best
that he not put too much emphasis on a uniform, either.
He brought back his identity card and his clearance from
Zirndorf. The older policeman examined them carefully.
"Your name is Konrad Molokan?" he said.

"Yes."

There was no other answer to give but Konrad had
never felt any sense of kinship with the name "Molokan."
Father Stephen had all of his records but Konrad was not
certain that they were authentic, or that Father Stephen
actually knew who he was. If papers were a need, the
monastery could, of course, supply them. It was a place
of much guile as well as of many skills. It might have
supplied his identity.

"Have you permission to live in these quarters?" the
policeman asked.

"No. I haven't. When I reached here yesterday there
were boys throwing rocks at the place. They broke that
window."

"So you decided to move in without permission?"

"I didn't know where to ask for permission."

"How about the lock? This place has always been
locked. Did you break the lock?"

"No. There wasn't any lock. Someone must have broken
it off and taken it away."

"We'll take a look at the place."

The two policemen, obviously, had never been in the structure before. Konrad followed them as they moved from room to room. The older policeman frowned in concentration trying to read the lettered sentence in the toilet room. He shook his head.

"Were you planning to live here?" he said.

"I would like to do that."

"You haven't any light. No stove or refrigerator or furniture."

Konrad smiled. "I never need much. I could get along without those things."

The big policeman relaxed noticeably. "It says in your papers that you are a Monk, a Russian Monk."

"That is correct."

"You should have no difficulty. You can easily find better places to live than this. There are two Russian churches in Munich."

"I like it here."

"Well, we can't give you permission to stay here. This property is leased by the United States Army."

The younger policeman spoke for the first time. He looked harder, more combative, than the older man. "The Americans hired their own guards for their other property," he said. "I don't believe it is our job to guard this."

The two men exchanged glances and reached agreement in those glances without resort to words. The issue was, suddenly and subtly, the matter of American responsibility for German soil on which Americans had erected facilities. The older man expelled a held breath.

"*Ja,*" he said.

He turned to Konrad then. "This is American property, this shed and the small plot of ground surrounding it. They can expel you from it. Because you are a religious

seeking shelter, we find no harm in you and we will not
report to the Americans."

His voice was stern but there was a friendly gleam in his
eye. "You must not light fires in the forest," he said, "not
for heat or for cooking or for any other purpose. If you
cause people to bring charges of any kind against you, you
will have to leave. Understand?"

"I understand. Thank you."

The younger man turned, walking back to the Volkswagen. The older man smiled, waved his hand and followed him. Konrad watched the police car drive away, remembering the desperate horde of people at Zirndorf. They
had been people from all over Europe, mainly from the
Iron Curtain countries. Konrad had talked with a Latvian
who said there was a large Latvian settlement at Würz-
burg, Latvians who had refused to return to a Communist-
ruled homeland after the war. There were similar pockets
of people all over Germany and the Germans had grown
accustomed to refugees. Such spots as the camping grounds
here on the edge of Munich were a hospitality.

It was too late to push the cart into town and seek out
people who might have family treasures to be repaired.
Konrad walked through his house with a fresh sense of
occupancy, almost of ownership. He was existing here now
by police fiat. He wished that his cart contained a broom
and a bucket. The house needed cleaning. He went outside.

Two youths were crossing the clearing. One of them
was yesterday's leader, Werner. His companion was the
thin lad who had had only one idea to express, his negative
impression of all Russian ancestry. They were tall young
men. Werner, despite his scowl, was a handsome youth:
high forehead, firm chin, thick dark hair. The other lad
slouched in his walk; sullen, slack-lipped, noticeably less
fit than Werner. Konrad stood outside of his door waiting

for them. Werner was the leader again, as he had been yesterday, the other youth dropping back, a few steps behind
him.

"We saw the police car," Werner said. "We want you to
know that we had nothing to do with it. We handle our
own trouble. We did not report you."

Konrad waved to the grassy stretch on the right of his
doorway approach. "We could sit down and talk it over,"
he said. "I would like to know why I am trouble to
you."

He sat on the grass without waiting for a reply. Werner
hesitated and the thin youth cursed. "All cops are sons of
bitches," he said, "and all priests."

Konrad nodded. "And all Russians," he said softly.

"You're damned right. All Russians!"

Werner waved his companion to silence and sat on the
grass. "You are trouble," he said, "because you are the
main office, the big plant, the writer of messages. You came
in here from nowhere yesterday, telling us what we could
do and couldn't do. We live here."

"You have a point when you put it that way. I'm not a
policeman. I was taught that I should add something to
the world out of my life, bring something with me that
was not here when I came. You were doing something
opposed to that. You were destroying. For no purpose.
You were taking something out of the world, something
that might serve someone else."

"A window in a whorehouse! That is all that you saw us
take out of the world. You want it in?"

"Yes. I'm living there. Who told you that it was a whorehouse?"

Werner shrugged. "Everybody knows that. Except
strangers! As I told you, you came in here acting like you

know everything. Well, you don't. You don't belong here. We do. That's why you are a trouble."

Konrad nodded his head slowly. "I can see that. You belong here. If I live here for a while, I'll belong here. I'm living in the house. What was it before it was a whore-house? Do you know?"

Werner frowned. There was concentration behind the tightening of his features. He could not admit any lack of knowledge now.

"The Americans had radio or something in that shack," he said. "Code stuff. Very secret. They moved out of the shack while they still had the place up on the hill. Up across the road that was. The whores moved into the shack when they left. The soldiers used to come across the road at night. They used to stand in line sometimes. There were only a few women; three, I think."

"We used to come out here and watch them," the thin youth said.

His voice was rather high-pitched. He seemed to be talking to himself or to the world at large rather than to Konrad. His eyes were alive, remembering, where they had been dull in contemplating the present.

"We used to lie on our bellies in the grass back of here and watch them," he said.

Konrad thought of the sign inside the house that read, HAIRY MARY. This was an area in which these boys were wiser, more knowledgeable than he. He had grown up without knowing that prostitution existed, without im-agining it. The Bible was explicit enough on the subject but the meaning had passed him by. He knew now only what he had learned secondhand in Vienna. He looked at Wer-ner, who knew much and little, who argued well.

"What were you trying to prove by breaking win-dows?" he said.

"Nothing. I don't have to prove anything."

"We all have to prove things; to ourselves if not to other people."

"I don't. I don't have to prove a damned thing."

There was strength in Werner. He made a statement and he let it lie. He had antagonism in his eyes and in his voice but he was willing to talk. That, Konrad felt, was a gain on his own part. These boys, apart from the policemen, were the only people whom he knew in Munich. Werner interested him and the thin youth did not interest him at all but he addressed himself to both of them.

"You belong here," he said. "You are not strangers. You made the point well. I need help from someone who belongs here. I am a restorer of things, of old paintings and carvings and jewelry, some musical instruments, many things. People would be suspicious of me, probably, because I am a stranger, but you know the people. I will share with you if you help me to find work to do."

Konrad was not certain that he needed help but it would be interesting to have someone work with him. He watched the boys and, surprisingly, it was the thin youth who answered him.

"You want old people," he said. "They are the ones who have things. Old people. We can't help you. Old people don't like us."

"That's right," Werner said. "Older people do not believe that anyone is any good until he is old. They expect everyone to be interested in the same stupid things. The world is not the way older people say it is."

"The people know you even if they don't like you. You said it yourself: you belong here."

"They don't care who we are."

"You don't know. There is beauty in people."

"There is poison in people, black, dirty poison." Werner

rose to his feet. "You go and find people yourself and fix their junk if you can fix it. I don't know if you can fix anything."

Konrad rose slowly. "There is a proverb in Russia," he said. "If you beat a Russian enough, he can do anything, even make a watch."

Werner did not smile. "I hate Russians," he said.

"You hate too many things. All of the things you hate will hate you. You will be outnumbered."

Werner shrugged and turned away. The other boy hesitated then spat at Konrad's feet. "You go to hell," he said.

He followed Werner and Konrad watched the two boys until they stepped through the green at the far side of the clearing. There had been hatred in the thin boy's eyes when he spat and there did not seem to be any reason for hatred. Hatred, of course, was always difficult to understand; it seemed to flow against life rather than with it.

Konrad carried his doubts and questions to his nightly hour of prayer but the voices beyond himself were still and nothing moved in his mind except a statement of Father Stephen's, a statement from a long time ago:

"If you have a problem," Father Stephen had said, "it was given to you for a purpose. You were meant to have it. Accept it and think about it."

Chapter Five

There was a soft rain in the night and the morning was drenched with it; misty rain blowing with an easy wind and sogging the ground underneath. A man could think of sound reasons for staying home with a cart that had to be pushed, but days such as this were good days for that very reason; a great many people stayed home.

Konrad pushed his cart, stopping conscientiously at door after door. He was a medieval figure in his black robe with the hood protecting his head. Most of the women who answered doors were abrupt with him, obviously suspicious of all that was unfamiliar about him: appearance, costume, the slight accent on certain German words. A dark-eyed woman, who wore her white hair like a cap, invited him in.

"There's a clock you might look at," she said. "It will take you out of the rain, looking at it."

"Thank you."

The house had only four rooms; a sparkling clean house with old, shabby furniture, most of which had not been good when new. There was a tall clock in a corner, a walnut case with a golden angel in the arch of the dial. Konrad took a step toward it but the woman waved him back.

"It will wait," she said. "It has waited for years. Have you had your lunch?"

"No."

"Good. You will have it with me. I will have a man for company. Come. Sit at the table while I bring it in."

There was a soup fragrance floating in the air. The woman set two places then brought in the tureen. She straightened when she set it down.

"I am Christa Clausen."

"I am Konrad, a Russian Monk."

She nodded. "You may say grace if you will. I am not very religious but I will try to follow."

Konrad stood before the table with his head bowed. He was glad to say thank you for this moment, for the fare that was a pleasant aroma in his nostrils, for this woman who had invited him in. He composed his prayer, as he liked to do, fitting it to the occasion, requiring nothing of Christa Clausen save an "Amen." When he sat across the table from her, the woman seemed amused. There was quiet laughter in her eyes. She had a wide mouth and a short nose, a pleasant woman.

"Tell me about yourself," she said. "I do not have many visitors."

"There is little to tell. My monastery is far away. I have no church. I fix things that need fixing. I prefer that they be beautiful things."

"Ah, yes. You would, of course. It is in your eyes. You have the eyes of a boy. Perhaps you do not know that. Do you think that my clock is beautiful?"

"I do. I hope that I can fix it. I have not had much experience with clocks."

The woman waved her hand. "I have changed my mind. I do not want it fixed. It would develop a personality. There is room for only one personality in this house."

"But I do not undrestand."

"Of course not. You are not a woman. I will bring you a slice of pie."

The woman, when she brought the pie, was suddenly formal, a bit withdrawn, no longer talkative. When Konrad rose to leave, she rose with him.

"It was a wonderful lunch," he said. "I have never tasted better soup. I would like to do something for you."

"You have. You cannot know about that." She walked before him to the door, then turned. Her smile was warm, a flash of white teeth under the wide lips. "Look! See what a good meal does for one. It even improves the weather."

The rain was no longer falling. There was blue in the sky behind a scattered cavalry troop of white cloud. Water dripped from the trees and ran in random rivulets under foot. The name of the street, Konrad noted, was Rockingerstrasse. He was not interested in names but he saw this one on a street sign. There were white and pink blossoms on the trees.

He noted another name after a long string of turnaways. He walked through a silent neighborhood of mainly dull red brick buildings. Some of the buildings had, obviously, been offices, some dormitories, some private residences. They were deserted now. Two squares away he saw a patrol on duty, German, protecting the property. This section, too, had belonged to the Americans. The name of the street on which he walked was Rockefellerstrasse.

The name "Rockefeller" was vaguely familiar to him. He associated it with oil and politics and movies. He found another series of occupied homes and another long list of refusals. No one had any work for him to do or, if they had it, did not trust him with it.

There was a broad highway with much traffic flowing

on it. On the far side there was a large army camp falling into ruin. The roofs of some of the buildings had collapsed and others sagged. There was a gate with a single guard on duty and a line of abandoned, rusting vehicles. A large sign read: ALABAMA KASERNE.

This, too, was American, or had been American.

Konrad did not cross the highway. He was a relatively long way from his headquarters and he turned back. The third stop on his return journey gained him an invitation to come in. It was a small house with flowers in a miniature garden, trees heavy with blossoms. The door was opened by a man, a short, frail, bald-headed man with deeply carved wrinkles in his face.

"Come in," he said. "I see little of the Church. I welcome having it come to me."

"I'm not the Church. I am a Russian Monk. I am looking for work to do."

"Russian, eh? Well, come in. I was one of the brutal Huns sent up to fight your people. You wouldn't think it now, would you. I was one of the lucky ones. I got wounded early. If I didn't I'd have spent ten or twenty years doing labor for you."

"Not for me. I know nothing about the war."

"Lucky. Very lucky. Like me, only different. No matter. Come in. What kind of work do you do?"

"Mostly I fix things, or restore them. I work in paint on metal or ivory or jade, in wood or canvas."

"Canvas? Can you restore a painting? Make it as it was?"

"That depends on how good the painting was and on what happened to it."

The man lighted his pipe. "It's not very good, I guess. It's my mother. There were artists who came around, just as you came today. We lived in Passau. Have you ever been in Passau?"

"No."

"Lovely place. Two rivers and the woods and the Cathedral on the hill. Mostly I remember the arches connecting the houses. Never mind. It was lovelier than here. My mother and my sister came here when I was in the army. They lived in this house. My sister put my mother's picture under the floor in this room. Nobody found it when they looted."

The man rose and walked into an adjoining room. He returned with a canvas in a damaged gilt frame. The canvas was two feet square.

"I can't see her any more," the man said. "She's faded out or hidden or something. I'd like to see her." He drew hard on his pipe. "She died while I was away in the army."

Konrad looked at the painting. It had gathered much dirt and soot while it was under the floor. He could dimly see the figure of a woman. This would be a difficult assignment. The itinerant artists who did family portraits did not paint for the ages. Their work was sometimes well done, more often not; a quick, light study with no expensive materials used.

"I don't suppose you can do anything with it," the man said.

Konrad's decision was made, listening to the voice behind the words. "Yes, I can," he said, "if I can take it with me. I couldn't work here."

The man hesitated, then waved one hand. "Take it," he said. "I'll trust you to bring it back. If you don't, I probably have little time in which to own things anyway."

"I'll bring it back. Let us wrap it."

The only wrapping available was newspaper and packaging the painting to the cart was awkward. The man stepped back and looked at it.

"I'll pay whatever it costs," he said. "You wouldn't think

it but I have a little money. I haven't any one but myself to spend on . . ."

Konrad thought about that, walking back to his place in the woods. There were so many people, mainly women, who had no one but themselves to spend on. That was what war did to people. Maybe, like the old man, an individual might have a little money. It was a poor substitute for all that he did not have.

Konrad bought sandwich meat and bread on his way home. He had had one hot meal for the day and the camping ground would be an inhospitable kitchen tonight. The earth was still soggy under his feet when he walked away from pavement. He was content within his walls when he reached them but it was too dark for examination of the portrait. That had to wait until morning.

The morning was bright and he set up his easel, an essential part of his cart equipment, in the center of the clearing, free from the shadow of the trees. The painting was very dark. The varnish film had deteriorated badly. Konrad put some solvent on cotton wool and tested it on the upper left-hand corner. He tried three different solvents before he found one that satisfied him. He had bottles and sealed cans wrapped into compartments in his cart, a wide assortment, and brushes of many kinds and sizes. He worked slowly, gently. It would be so easy to remove the painting with the varnish.

The work of this unknown wandering artist was not, he knew, worth the effort that it demanded of him but there was a fascination in the difficulty that it presented and it was his first work in Germany. The old man who had given him this work to do had imparted a special value to the work, the sentimental value that the painting held for him.

There was a woman looking out of the canvas at 2:15, a

younger woman than Konrad had anticipated. She was still
a dim figure but he could read expression in her face. The
painter had painted her as she was, not glorifying her or
endowing her with artificial prettiness. She had dark hair
and large eyes, exceptionally large eyes. She was bending
forward slightly and her hair was parted on the left side,
just a trifle left of center. She had a soft vulnerable mouth
and she was not relaxed.

Konrad felt someone behind him, someone looking over
his shoulder. He spoke without trying to identify the in-
truder, more interested in the woman than in the leaning
person.

"See," he said, "she is worried. She wants to look her
best and she is afraid that she does not look well. Her husband probably employed that painter. He didn't give her
time to get ready."

"How do you know so much about women?"

He looked up, recognizing the voice. Werner was laughing at him. The boy was attractive when he laughed.
Konrad waved his hand.

"I know nothing of women," he said. "I know a little of
art, of portraits."

It was the truth. He would not, he was certain, see as
much in the face of a living woman as he saw in the woman
of the portrait. This artist was better, or potentially better, than he had anticipated, driven probably to the use of
cheap materials by the same poverty, or misfortune, or
perversity, which had made him a painter of parlor art. The
woman he had painted was living again as she had lived on
that day when he posed her.

"You really do work, don't you?" Werner said.

"Certainly."

"Can you paint portraits?"

"No."

"I think I could."

"Could you?" Konrad reached into a portfolio at his feet for sketch pad and two pencils. "Do one of me," he said.

Werner accepted the pad and sat on the grass. Konrad focused his attention once more upon the woman. She was wearing a blue dress, a soft material, a house dress, with an open collar that had a red design in it, a deep red, maroon. She was a woman who did her own hair. She was, perhaps, in her thirties. Konrad had no confidence in his ability to judge accurately the age of a woman. This one looked tired as well as anxious. She probably worked hard. It was strange that her husband would have her portrait painted like this. It had to be her husband's decision. She would dress for it, even if she had little in which to dress, dress as she would for church.

No. It wasn't strange, actually. This man was a German husband. He loved his wife or he would not want a portrait of her. He wanted her to look as he was accustomed to seeing her. He loved her as she was every day and that was how he wanted her on the canvas.

The woman was emerging clearly now. She had not looked directly at the artist; she had looked past and beyond him, at something behind his left shoulder as he faced her. It was all quite clear to Konrad as he worked, the people alive and involved in living: woman, husband, artist. The house in which they lived was shadowy, not because of aging varnish but because the artist had seen it that way, less important than the woman; not worth his effort to fill in detail.

"I have finished with you. There you are."

Werner's voice had triumph in it. He had done something that he had said he would do and he was happy with the result. He walked across the clearing and flipped the sketch pad into Konrad's lap. It was a casual gesture but his voice was not casual. Konrad looked at the sketch.

There was a man working at an easel, a man with a prominent straight nose and prominent cheekbones, with a strong chin, a large mouth and two bracket lines curving around that mouth: a lean, hungry-looking man with intent eyes. Konrad, who shaved with the sense of touch rather than the sense of sight, did not see himself often but this was a good sketch.

"You did that well," he said. "Where did you learn to do that?"

"We had a course in school. It's something I liked to do."

"You have a talent. You could develop it."

"Why should I?"

"Talents should not be wasted. Maybe this is what you were meant to do."

"You have more art talent than I have. You know how to do a lot of things that I would have to learn. What good is it? You do not have anything. You do not make as much money as my father who works in a factory."

"Is your father happy working in a factory?"

"No."

"I am happy doing what I do."

Werner walked a few steps away from the easel, a few steps back. "You won't stay happy," he said. "It makes no sense, doing what you do. It can't last. It doesn't go anywhere. I don't see what you stand for. You don't even stand for religion."

"What does go somewhere? What do you think I should do? What will you do?"

"I don't know. That's the hell of it, the living hell of it. If I could see what to do, I'd do it."

Konrad wiped his hands. He sat on the ground, facing

the boy who had already dropped down, and who was sitting cross-legged. "You go to school, I would imagine," he said slowly. "Well, that is what you do. You learn all you can and prepare for the future, for whatever you get a chance to do."

"Do you know what I study, the kind of a future that I have?"

"No."

The simple "No" had to stand without elaboration. Konrad could not imagine a German school, or any school. He had never been in a schoolroom and he did not know what was taught at the various ages. He was aware of great gaps in his own knowledge and he assumed that these gaps were solid spaces in the knowledge patterns of others. On the other hand he knew many things, and had many resources. There was no way of measuring what he had learned for comparison with the learning of others, but he had no point of vantage on which to stand in discussing education.

"I study French and English and Latin," Werner said, "and I study biology and mathematics and natural science. I study German literature, and I have a course in art."

"It sounds good. Why are you complaining?"

"I am from a poor family. I must earn money. Will good grades in those subjects get a job for me?"

"Education isn't for getting jobs."

"What else is there? For someone like me, I mean."

"What do you want?"

"You asked that before. I don't know. I know that I don't want what my father has."

"What does your father have?"

"He has a job in a factory. A razor-blade factory. He helps to make razor blades. He wants to get me a job there. It is the only place where he has influence. How about that. You don't make razor blades with French and Latin and biology and all that stuff. Why don't people like me just learn to make razor blades and nothing else?"

"You have a talent for drawing. You might do something with that."

"What?"

"I don't know. In five or seven years, if you worked at it, I would know. So would you."

Werner jumped impatiently to his feet. "I haven't got five or seven years," he said.

He turned and strode away without looking back. Konrad watched him go, sympathizing with him. The boy had a problem and he stated it well. What did one do with the learning of classrooms? How did one discover an end and an aim in life if the end and the aim were not inherent in the way of life that was his? Konrad, who knew nothing of classrooms and little of the work that men did, felt helpless in the presence of Werner.

"He has character," he said. "He will help himself better than I can ever help him."

He turned his attention back to the canvas on his easel. The woman was looking out at him through a faint mist. She was a patient woman. He was certain of that. She had not had an easy life but she had a husband who loved her, who had her portrait painted. Her son, like this boy Werner, did not have any place to go. He had been taken into the army and wounded. He was an old man now and he did not seem to have much. It was difficult to advise people about living, about life. Very difficult.

The light was fading. He wrapped the painting gently and took it into the house. It was too much trouble to walk to the camping ground and fix a hot meal. He had bread and cheese and lunch meat in the house. He ate that slowly, not thinking about anything. When the dark closed in, he went out to pray.

He stood for a moment, breathing the night air and somewhere in his mind he could hear the voice of Father Stephen, saying what he had said a long time ago.

"When you do not understand another person," Father Stephen said, "look inward to yourself and your own life for the understanding. It is there."

Chapter Six

It was one of the great fulfillments of life to sit on the ground under the stars, or a cloudy sky, or a brilliant moon, whatever one had, and let prayer flow into one; not to send prayer out, nor recite prayer, nor compose it, merely to breathe it in, feeling beyond all doubt the companionship that came with the prayer. One accepted what came to him; one did not attempt to shape the hour or dictate what went into it.

The last few nights had been quiet nights, wrapped in peace but without images. No answers had come to Konrad, no glow of wisdom, no bright light of truth. Tonight was different. The night was without stars and there was a cloud curtain over the moon. He moved out of himself, out of the night, into a night that had passed into history, living that night again as he had lived it in its moment, its succession of moments.

It had been cold in the big railroad station. People moved swiftly. There was a confusion of sound. Konrad walked beside Father Stephen who seemed to bulk and tower over him. "Keep your head down. Do not call attention to yourself," Father Stephen said.

There was nervousness in the big priest's voice and that

was a very rare thing. There was, of course, an excuse for it tonight. Konrad kept his head pulled down under his cowl, his shoulders pulled up. He was one of six Monks on their way to Dresden in East Germany, a six selected for their skills in restoring works of art. The Soviet Government had ordered six and the Abbot of the monastery had selected the men.

Of the six men, huddled together on the icy platform, only Father Stephen was unqualified in terms of hand skills, but he was a Monk of Monks, a man with the gift of command. Konrad was sixteen years old, the possessor of many skills but without existence as a Monk or as a person. Stephen had smuggled him into the monastery long ago and he had grown there, a secret shared by many Monks and betrayed by none of them. Konrad had papers of a kind, papers prepared by men who understood the paper work of an autocratic bureaucracy, but he did not belong in the world where young men had certain school classifications and a liability to army duty. That was the world into which he stepped when he left the shelter of the monastery walls.

"We can take no chances until we are in Germany," Stephen said, "and few chances there. You must not answer questions."

Konrad had given no thought to answering questions. He had, however, wanted to grow a beard, or attempt to grow one. Stephen had been curt in his rejection of the idea. "You are not a priest and you cannot wear a beard," he said. There were Monks with beards in the monastery who were not priests and Konrad was the only beardless Monk, but Stephen's word, when he pronounced it, was the law.

No one asked questions. The six Monks rode the train to the border and a couple of pompous but indifferent

officials examined their papers. Monks, obviously impov-
erished and moving from one controlled situation into another were of slight interest.

Konrad found the trip exciting. A foreign country was
an abstraction, something about which he might read in
a book but not anything that he ever expected to see.
East Germany, of course, was part of Russia but the people
would be Germans. There was very little in the monastery
library about the great war between Germany and Russia.
There was, in fact, amazingly little genuine history. Father
Stephen had dismissed the importance of history with a
wave of his hand.

"The people of God are divided into nations," he said,
"but one should not learn to think of nations as friends or
enemies. Nations are people and people, wherever they
live, are the Creatures of God."

Dresden, when they reached it, was gloomy and depress-
ing. They saw little of the city and that little needed re-
construction. They were carried in a truck to a big warehouse, painfully new and without any gracious or lovely
touches. They had small cell-like rooms with plain hard
beds such as they had in their home monastery. There
were other Monks who had been assembled for this assignment from various regions of Russia, from Czechoslovakia,
two from Bulgaria. There were Germans, too, but they
were museum-trained workers, not Monks.

Dresden had been one of the most brutally bombed cities
in the history of the world . . . 650,000 incendiary bombs
had been dropped on the city in a single night and in the
morning over three hundred American bombers blasted
it with high explosive bombs. Some 135,000 people died
and great art treasures perished. More than a dozen years
later, an attempt was being made to redeem from rubble
some of the beauty that had been destroyed. Crews of

Germans had worked for years to sort and classify bits and pieces from wreckage. The bits and pieces waited as a challenge to Monk restorers.

Konrad was the youngest Monk on the project but not the least skilled. He had given his life to God and to this work early because there was nothing else to which he could give his life. He had an instinctive feeling about a broken piece which had been the part of a greater whole; he could see as inevitable a pattern into which the piece fitted. He knew from experience how to use glues and resins, cements and wax. He worked patiently with cracks in pottery and porcelain and breaks in china. He could carve in wood to replace missing members of a figure or group of figures. He had been assistant to the glass repairer at the monastery, a Monk who could mend broken glass, eradicate nicks and blemishes, do incredible magic in restoring vases, decanters, ornaments, or panels. Konrad had never been allowed to do the work but he had watched while such highly demanding work was done.

In Dresden he was the perpetual assistant, assisting often some gruff, grumpy, disagreeable Monk less skillful than himself or some cheerful faker who seemed to be more of an artist than he was. One met all kinds of men and adapted to them in humility.

He worked a year and a half in Dresden. In March of 1961, a message came to Father Stephen from Russia. Konrad never knew who sent the message nor how it was delivered. He remembered discussing it at night in the deep basement where great canvases were stretched and paintings re-created. There were three men: Father Stephen, another Monk, and himself. It was dark and there was a heavy odor but no one could approach them without sending a warning of sound ahead of him.

"Khrushchev is turning a reasonable face to the world,"

Father Stephen said, "but he is purging the monasteries and the Church of those who had any favor with Stalin. Many of our friends have disappeared into the catacombs or merely disappeared. We are fortunate that we were not in line when the axe fell but we have little time."

Father Dmitri, a short stocky priest who had taught Konrad Latin and French and some understanding of Byzantine art, was the third member in the basement. "You had no favors from Stalin," he said, "nor I."

"We survived under Stalin and Basil ran the monastery with a shrewd hand, offending no one. Basil is vulnerable now through us, through Konrad."

"He always has been."

"Yea. But next week three officials are coming here. They are not looking for a specific something; they are looking for anything that can be used against the Church and the monasteries. We cannot afford to be here, Konrad and I."

"Do you believe that you can get away?"

"Yes. There is a man, a genius in tapestry, a German. You know him. He belongs to a catacomb. More East Germans are leaving than is admitted. They escape every night."

"Germans, yes. Russians, no. And Dresden is not Berlin. It is more difficult from here."

"It is not impossible."

Konrad listened respectfully but his nerves tightened. A Monk was permitted moral heroism, but empty heroic gestures were frowned upon. When one was young, one dreamed of empty heroic gestures, savoring them, considering them good. This was a moment worthy of a knight, with or without armor.

"I will go alone," he said. "It will be easier."

"You would not get out of Dresden," Stephen said.

"I speak German well. I would have a chance."

Father Dmitri leaned forward. He was younger than Father Stephen but looked older. He had three curving lines of wrinkles beneath each eye and an upended funnel of wrinkles above the bridge of his nose. His beard was thin and wiry, untidily kept, a mixture of black and gray.

"You would have no chance," he said. "You are too young. You belong, too, with Stephen. He gave up his own life for you when you were a baby, coming to the one place where you would be safe and anchoring his living to that place."

"Pouff!" Stephen said. "I am a man of impulse. My own will acted. He owes me nothing."

Konrad was accustomed to this, discussions which ignored his presence even when they concerned him.

"I know very little about myself," he said.

"No need to know." Stephen's voice was gruff. "The only thing that matters is that we leave here. Not an hour more here than we must spend. I confide in you, Dmitri, because you are a conspirator by nature. You will know of approaches to this German underground."

"I know two."

"Will they act for blessings when we have no money?"

"They will act from a love of danger." Dmitri paused. "I, of course, will go with you."

"No, Dmitri. You have no reason."

The short Monk smiled. "Say that I, too, love danger," he said.

It was only 110 miles to Berlin but that was a complicated place in which too many people were crossing into West Germany and too many were being caught. The thirty miles from Dresden to the Czechoslovakian border were fraught with danger but, so the catacomb people said, it was not so difficult to get into Czechoslovakia.

Not too many people tried it because an East German saw no advantage to himself in leaving his own country for Czechoslovakia where Germans were unpopular.

"We are Russians and we may be unpopular, too, in Czechoslovakia," Father Stephen said, "but we will risk it."

They went out of the warehouse on the evening of April first, the feast of Saint Macarius, the wonder-worker. They rode in the bottom of a truck which carried sacks of debris. It was difficult to breathe but the sacks had been cunningly stacked and did not weigh on them. Monks were considered safe workers of predictable habits so there were no guards at the warehouse. At the outskirts of Dresden, the four men—including the tapestry expert who wanted ultimately to reach West Germany—slept for three hours in the barn of a catacomb conspirator. They crept out in the darkest, quietest hour of night. There was a big field, a road, a wall with lights strung on it.

Konrad felt again that thrill of adventure. Another foreign country lay behind those lights. His nerves were tight wires under his skin. He moved in a crouch as the others did, well out of the range of the lights. Their farmer guide led them east and south as he said that he would. There was a field that had been flooded, turned into a veritable swamp, as a cheap means of discouraging refugees from attempting the border illegally.

"You could drown easily in there," the man said, "but there is a way."

The way was a causeway of stone, hidden in the water but a safe passage if one were careful. It was a mile southeast of the lighted gate.

"It is not perfectly straight. There are zags in it. Watch for them," the farmer said. "Good luck to you."

The tapestry man led with Dmitri second, Konrad third,

and Stephen in the rear. It was gingerly walking at first but as their confidence built, they moved more swiftly, keeping distance from the man ahead as an added precaution. They would come out of the flooded land on the Czech side, the farmer told them, and there would be no causeway for the last hundred yards or, perhaps, two hundred.

The powerful spotlight hit them without warning, shooting out of some staked-out spot just east of where they were. It caught the tapestry man, outlining him sharply. Father Dmitri, too, was boldly outlined. Father Stephen's hands were as swift as the light. He lifted Konrad off the stone path and dropped with him into the water.

The tapestry man made two leaps forward then plunged out of sight. Father Dmitri seemed paralyzed. He stood frozen, staring at the light, then made some kind of a gesture with his right hand. A rifleman, from behind the light, shot him.

Konrad saw that much and then he was lying flat in the swamp, partly supported by a thrusting bar of stone, submerged so that only his face was above water. He breathed with difficulty but he breathed. Stephen, he knew, was close to him but he did not know exactly where. The light had swung south, looking for the tapestry man, and the men behind the light obviously believed that there had been only two would-be escapees.

There were no more shots or shouts, so they evidently had failed to locate the tapestry man. Konrad heard them splashing back through the water and he held his breath. They were speaking German, cursing emotionally. They found Father Dmitri's body. Konrad had never doubted that he was dead. They commented on the body then carried it away. They had a trophy and that, in a sense, seemed to satisfy them. Konrad heard the splashing grow fainter and fainter then it ceased.

He worried about Father Stephen, lying there in the water, but he had more confidence in the priest than he had in himself. He did not want to bring the guards back, or their light, so he did not speak. It was a long wait and the chill soaked into him; finally Father Stephen's voice came to him, a thin whisper.

"Are you all right?"

"Yes."

"We'll go on then while we have the dark."

Father Stephen rose out of the water like some big ungainly animal. He swerved from side to side as he struggled upright on the stone causeway. Once upright, he bent forward and crouched again. He seemed to have trouble in taking the first step. Konrad understood that. He was very cold, too, and it was difficult to move his legs. The stone was slippery under his feet. He saw Father Stephen achieve control over himself and move forward. He could do no less but there was a numbness in his legs. He did not dare stumble for fear the noise would bring the light again. Stephen moved faster than he did, drawing away from him. It was a long slow journey.

He was grateful that the night was dark. Rain fell, thinly at first then with greater volume and in greater force. It was difficult to see and he lost Stephen. Panic rose in him but he kept on, not letting himself hurry, putting one foot down and then the other, setting them precisely on the slippery stone. Then the stone path ended. His breath caught as he stepped off into water that almost reached his waist.

He thought for a moment that he had taken a wrong step but he remembered that they had been told in advance about this ending of the causeway. He would have to walk now for a hundred yards, or two hundred, through the water.

It was closer to two hundred. The night was deep dark and the rain came steadily, slanting slightly. The water was shallow now, barely over his ankles and there was a bank ahead of him. Father Stephen was lying on his stomach, peering down into the water. He stretched out his hand when he saw Konrad and Konrad came up to him.

"You were slow," Stephen said. "You're an older man than I am."

His teeth were chattering and he stuttered, which robbed his speech of both rebuke and jest. Konrad was shivering, too. His clothes clung wetly to him and the rain beat against him.

"We can move in a bit farther," Father Stephen said. "Not very far. We have to see where we're going."

They walked, stumbling on rough muddy ground. There was no sign of a path or a road or a structure of any kind. Despite his statement that they could not go very far, Stephen seemed anxious to get away from the swamp. They had put distance behind them when they saw the trees, a forest of trees. There was cover, concealment, a measure of protection from the rain. They sank to the ground gratefully, their backs to a broad trunk.

"I wish I'd thought to bring some brandy," Father Stephen said.

Konrad had never tasted brandy but he knew that it reputedly warmed a man's blood. He thought about that, his body shaking with the cold. They were, undoubtedly, in Czechoslovakia. The people might be anything; Russians or Russian-disciplined or free souls. He doubted that they would be free souls. They could, of course, be rebels. That thought held possibilities. He rose and walked back and forth, fighting the cramping in his legs. Father Stephen did not move so he stood over him.

"Are you all right?" he said.

"Yes. All right."

The older man's voice was hoarse. He was not all right. The first light of dawn, making its way hesitantly across the rain-swept country, revealed a dull-eyed Father Stephen whose face had a gray look. Konrad spoke to him and he did not answer. His pulse seemed weak and he obviously had neither the will nor the strength to move away from the tree, nor the awareness of need or necessity. Konrad looked at him helplessly. Stephen was too big and too heavy to carry and if one could carry him, there was no place to take him.

"I can't just stand here," Konrad said.

He stood motionless, holding that thought. He was in a strange country on a cold, rainy morning and Father Stephen was unconscious. Father Stephen would have told him what to do but, alone, he did not know. He knew only that if he did not obtain help, Father Stephen would die. It was the first time in his life that he had been alone, completely alone with a decision to make.

He moved mechanically away from the trees, not choosing direction. He had walked less than twenty yards when he saw a house and farm buildings at the far end of a big narrow field. He hurried toward it, aware that it might shelter people who would be enemies to Father Stephen and himself. He had no choice but he prayed as he forced his legs across the wet earth.

There was a man crossing the space between the barn and the house. He stopped when he saw Konrad and waited for him, his eyes narrowed. He was a man in his fifties, medium tall, a man with a thrusting chin and a tight mouth. He did not move as Konrad approached and he waited for Konrad to speak first.

"I need help," Konrad said. "My companion is an old man. I had to leave him there under those trees. He's unconscious."

"Came out of Germany, did you?"

"Yes."

"Was that you they were shooting at last night?"

"Yes. They killed one of us."

The man seemed unimpressed. He looked over toward the distant trees. "Maybe you didn't improve yourself coming over here," he said. "No matter. I'll look at the man."

He went into the house briefly, then into one of the outbuildings. He came out with a heavy two-wheeled pushcart. "You push it," he said.

He strode out ahead and Konrad had difficulty with the clumsy cart. He was aware that he had referred to Father Stephen as an old man. He had never done that before, had never thought of him as old. The route that the farmer took was over higher ground, a curving ridge that provided solid traction. They came to the trees and the man bent over Stephen.

"What is he?" he asked.

It was obvious that he would ask, or comment. Father Stephen had a large crucifix suspended from a chain around his neck.

"He is a priest."

The man grimaced. "Are you a priest, too?"

"No. I am a Monk."

"Too young to be a priest probably. This is a sick man, a very sick man. I could take care of him."

"I have very little money."

"I'll talk terms with you. Let us take him back."

Together they lifted Stephen into the cart. Konrad

tried to push it but his strength was giving out. The farmer took it from him and pushed it, loaded, at a faster pace than Konrad had managed when it was empty. They came to the house and there was a woman standing in the doorway, a heavy woman as hard in appearance as the man. He spoke to her and she came out to look at Stephen. Together they took him into the house and laid him on a bed in a rear bedroom.

"I see my share of you fellows coming over the border," the man said. "I can get in trouble. Some I help, some I don't. Some I turn in to keep my reputation with the authorities. I haven't made up my mind about you yet."

"It wouldn't be good for us to go back."

"It never is. I'll make you an offer, take it or leave it. You can live here, and the old priest. We'll nurse him. My wife will. He'll get better maybe. I don't know. I have a big farm here. Too much for me. You work with me till we have a crop in the fall. I'll point you then to where you want to go and you can go."

The man watched Konrad's face through slitted eyes, his own face expressionless. Konrad did mental arithmetic. This was the spring and he would work as a laborer until fall. He had a free choice that was not a choice. He laughed softly. The joke was on him but, in its way, it was a funny joke.

"I'll work for you," he said.

The man nodded. "You didn't get much sleep last night and you're as wet as the old man. You'll be no good to me if you're sick. Have your breakfast and get to bed. We'll start you to work in the morning."

Sitting on the ground in West Germany, with trees around him and Munich within walking distance, Konrad relived that moment in all its wetness and weariness; then the film in his mind grew dim. There had been a summer, a long summer, in which he had worked like an animal and slept like an animal, knowing nothing of what was happening in Germany or in Russia, caring less. Father Stephen had had pneumonia, or something very close to it; in his recovery he had grown old, capable only of light work and given to long hours of silence, of staring into nothingness.

The film flickered out and Konrad rose slowly. He was not certain of what the prayer had told him, not certain that he could read his own life well.

"Every boy should have a Father Stephen in his life," he said.

The statement seemed inadequate. There was more to it than that. He shook his head. Nothing more came to him. He went slowly into the house.

Chapter Seven

The morning had a soft breeze that carried fragrance. There were pink blossoms and white at all the points of the compass. Konrad walked to the bathhouse then pushed his cart into the winding streets below it. There was a small house with a slanting roof of orange, a house with an immense chestnut tree dwarfing it. The chestnut was one of the few trees Konrad thought of with a name. It was the tree that, in blossom time, was trimmed with candles.

The woman who opened the door was old, a white-haired woman in a dark blue dress. She wore a pin with a pirouetting ballet dancer on it. Her eyes were kind and she did not seem to consider it odd that a young Monk was offering to fix any of her treasures which needed fixing. Her house had no obvious treasures. The furniture was ordinary, well-worn, shabby.

"I do have something. I do not know if you can fix it," she said. "Do you fix swords?"

"It depends on what has happened to the sword."

"I'll show you."

She was tiny and, obviously, had never been robust. A sword was an incongruous touch. She came back, carrying it; a small sword with a gilt steel hilt that was decorated with military figures. The blade had been broken loose from the hilt.

"It belongs in my family," she said, "and I am all that is left of the family. We belong together, that sword and me. I managed to keep it through the trouble."

Konrad turned the sword in his hand. It was a symbol of this woman's family. They had not been among the lowly. "I can fix it," he said, "but not with anything I have in my cart."

She looked into his eyes, then nodded. "I can trust you," she said. "Take it with you. Have you had lunch?"

He had not had lunch. She served him stew and she talked of many things but, strangely, not of herself. When he left her, he was well fed and, more important, he carried a sword that was a symbol of someone's trust in him, someone who knew nothing about him.

He stopped in a large garage where he could borrow the tools that he needed and he fixed the sword, anchoring the blade firmly once more to the hilt. He was working on the portrait of the woman when the boys came, sitting in his own clearing with the light flowing over his shoulder. Werner had the tall boy with him, the boy whose conversation was limited, in the main, to expletives. He was a sullen, unpleasant youth with dark hollows in his cheeks and downward curves in the corners of his mouth. Konrad ignored Werner momentarily, concentrating his attention on this youth.

"I don't know your name," he said.

"Why in hell should you?"

"You're a visitor."

"His name is Otto," Werner said. "He doesn't like his name."

"It's a good name." Konrad turned his head toward

Werner. "What brings you back? I thought that you went away angry at something."

"I want to watch you work on the painting. I told Otto about it."

"You're welcome. I may bore you. I have reached a delicate point. I won't talk to you."

Facing his canvas, Konrad thought momentarily about Werner. It was strange that the boy had returned as he did. There was hostility in him yet but it was not the rock-throwing, window-breaking hostility of their first meeting. Otto probably had changed little. He seemed a mere follower of Werner with no sharply defined character of his own.

The woman looked out of the canvas on his easel. She was not a beautiful woman, had probably never been a beautiful woman, but she was lovely. She did not know that she was lovely. She was worrying, he was certain, because she did not look at her best, or did not believe that she did. Konrad could understand why her husband wanted her portrait painted. He found himself liking the woman, liking her very much.

There were faded spots in the paint, some peeling over the left shoulder and in the spot where her hair dropped to her forehead above her right eye. Konrad tested his paint carefully. He always bought the best brushes; if he could not afford the best, he did without any. He had red sable brushes in various sizes and he had some fine camel's-hair brushes which were, of course, cow hair.

The boys were still there when he leaned back in his portable stool, satisfied with what he had done. They were sitting on the grass, behind him and to his right.

"I can see why you took so much time," Werner said.

"Can you? Why did I?"

"You weren't doing your own work. You had to match another man's work."

"Yes. That is perceptive of you. Which do you think was more difficult, the other man's work or mine?"

"The other man's."

"I am afraid that you are right."

The boy had been honest; and he had spoken truth, of course. It was the humbling thought with which a restorer, no matter how capable, had to live. He did not create anything. The other man, whether his work was fine or crude, was the creator; the restorer, even if he improved upon the work, was a mechanic of sorts, something less than an artist.

"What does it get you?"

Otto's voice broke in upon the thought, a harsh voice with the uneven rhythm of hoarseness in it. Konrad looked at him.

"What do you mean?"

"Just what I said. What does it get you? You learned how to do that. You did it. Who pays you?"

"There is an old man who owns the picture. I work for him while I work on it."

"Wealthy man?"

"No."

Otto laughed. It was not a pleasant laugh. "So that's what I asked. What does it get you? You live in this crummy whorehouse, you eat any kind of garbage, you look like a Goddamn beggar. Why should anybody learn to do what you do?"

There was a fire and eloquence in Otto that Konrad had never suspected. The boy was leaning forward, his fists clenched. There was a reality about him that Konrad had never sensed before. Otto had always seemed a limp, spineless individual with a limited vocabulary, a limited field of ideas. Despite the harsh personal verdict, Konrad liked Otto as he was now. It was the first time that he had ever liked him.

"You cannot measure everything by the yardstick of money," he said.

Otto did not change expression. "What else?"

"Look," Werner said. "This is what Otto means. We go to school. Everybody says we've got to work hard and amount to something. So we study Latin and we will never do anything where we use it. We study French and we won't ever go to France. Where do we go? We go to a factory and we get a job standing beside a machine. It's waiting for us."

Konrad stared at him. He had never been a boy himself, nor lived a boy's life. He had never faced the future as these boys were facing it because his future had seemed a part of his present and of his past. There had never been any alternatives for him to consider. He had not rebelled against what he had nor against what might await him. He did not know what men did in a factory but he was certain that their work was necessary to the welfare of other men and was, therefore, good in itself. He could not explain how he thought, or what he believed, to these boys because they were so entirely different. He spread his hands apart, a gesture of bewilderment, then drew them together again.

"You ignore God," he said. "He created you. He puts beauty in the world. He expects you to do the work that he sends to you and to find beauty in it."

"Did you ever see the smoke coming out of a factory chimney?" Otto asked. "What's beautiful about that?"

Werner turned away. "Ah, let him alone," he said. "He hasn't got any answers."

He walked across the clearing with Otto following him

and Konrad let them go. He had a sense of defeat. These boys had expected answers from him and he had failed them. He told himself that he did not have answers for Werner and Otto because the answers in his own mind were not answers that would have meaning for them. He did not understand their lives or their problems or their rebellion against the work in a factory to which they felt committed or condemned.

He took the painting into the house. It needed a night in which to dry.

There were no answers for him when he sat alone in the darkness and surrendered himself to silent prayer. Nothing came to him; no vision, no memory, no parable told in terms of his own life.

The painting was dry in the morning and he wrapped it carefully before he carried it to the small house behind the miniature garden. The short, frail bald-headed man opened the door and there was eagerness in his face, in his eyes.

"I thought that you would come today," he said. "I felt it. Could you do anything with the painting?"

"Judge that for yourself."

Konrad tore the paper and held the painting chest high. The man stared at it, his eyes wide, then sank slowly to his knees.

"My mother!" he said. "That's my mother. That's how she looked when I was a boy. That's how she looked, just like that."

There were tears running into the deep wrinkles of the man's face. "I never saw her after I went in the army," he said. "Never went home."

"Didn't you get a leave?"

"One. I was young. I was away from home. It was a short leave. You know how it was. I didn't go. I was a fool. Then I got wounded . . ." He made a dismissing gesture. "She looked like that."

"She was a lovely woman," Konrad said.

"She was. She was a gentle woman. Not very strong. She'd be alive yet if she got enough to eat. It was bad in Munich even for strong people. She wasn't strong."

He was crying softly and suddenly he stopped. "You brought her back to me," he said. "I'd give my house, everything I own, for that. It is a miracle. You brought her out of darkness. I'll pay you anything I have."

There was a decent price to ask for work and a charitable price for people who could not afford what they needed, and a piratical price that took advantage of a weak human moment. Konrad named the decent price and he would not allow the man to double it.

Outside on the street again he walked happily. There were rewards in the life that he lived. Doubts came to a man, and fears, and loneliness, but his work repaid him richly for the effort that he gave to it, and in coin that no one could steal from him. He looked at the trees in blossom on both sides of the roadlike street. The sun touched the blossoms, calling out the color, and a slight breeze moved them gently. All of these trees and blossoms belonged to him, a humble passer-by as fully as they did to those who owned or occupied the plots of ground on which they grew.

There was a cluster of women in front of a house where two streets crossed. He remembered the house. A most unpleasant woman lived there. Everyone in this neighborhood had been suspicious of him except one woman but this woman on the corner had been the most antagonistic, a sharp-tongued woman. As he drew close the women became aware of him and two of them stepped aside. There was another woman, a stranger, sitting on the sidewalk with her back to the fence.

"A Russian, like you are," one of the women said. "She should be in a hospital. God knows what disease she has."

The woman who leaned against the fence raised her head. She looked up at Konrad. Her face was flushed and there was a watery film in her eyes. She spoke in Ruthene-tinged Russian.

"I do not want to go to a German hospital," she said. "I am afraid."

There was pleading in her voice. The women obviously did not understand her. They were no longer paying any attention to her, they were watching Konrad's face. He spoke in Ukrainian to the woman.

"What is the matter with you?"

"I don't know. I am ill. I do not want to go to a German hospital."

"Where do you come from?

She waved the question aside with one hand then covered her face again, her palms against the skin. Konrad looked around the circle of eyes. "Who is she?"

"A stranger. Nobody knows her," one of the women answered. "She came out here on a trolley car, looking for Mrs. Lindner. Mrs. Lindner moved away a year ago. She went to Frankfurt. This woman is very ill. She should be in a hospital."

The stranger lifted her head. "Please, Father," she said, "do not let them put me in a German hospital."

He knew then, as he had suspected earlier, that she understood German. She could probably speak it. She had called him "Father." Many people did. His black robe suggested the priesthood, of course. He wanted to retreat from this situation. He did not want to be involved. His life was simple as it was and he had had a good day. This woman could be anything. She could be someone dangerous, or only a displaced person, a Stateless creature such as he had been himself. He thought, looking at her, of the parable of the Good Samaritan. There had been someone lying by the side of the road. One of those who passed by, offering no help, had been a priest. He looked at the group of people surrounding him. It had grown larger. On the outskirts of the crowd was Otto. Konrad drew a deep breath.

"I will take care of her," he said. "I will take her to my place." He raised his voice. "Otto, get me a wagon or a truck or something so that I can move this woman."

It was a command, confidently given, but he had no faith in Otto. Werner, if he were here, might be resourceful. He dropped on one knee beside the woman, aware of the voices that expressed shock and astonishment at the idea of a man, a man of the cloth even if Russian, taking an ill woman into his house, the place where he lived alone, a woman from God-knows-where. One feminine voice rose high above the others, angry, imperative.

"Otto, no! You must not have anything to do with this man, or the woman."

The woman on the ground had a fever and her pulse was jumpy, irregular. Konrad rose and a heavily built woman bore down on him, shaking a fist that was as big as that of a sturdy man.

"I will not have you leading my son into trouble," she said. "I have told him to stay away from you."

He could not see Otto. Konrad stood straight. "He will not get into trouble," he said. His eyes swept the group of women. "I am a Monk," he said, "a humble servant of God, but His servant. If you see evil in my caring for the sick, then you are evil."

The voices were quieted. Some of the eyes were friendly and some were not. He did not know if Otto was trying to find a vehicle for him or if Otto had merely run away. On the basis of his past impressions of Otto, running away would seem in character. A hand touched his forearm. He looked down into the dark eyes of the woman named Christa Clausen, the woman with a clock that did not tell time, the woman who had served him soup.

"Konrad, don't do it," she said softly. "Monk or not, do not take a woman into your house, not any woman."

"I must. You see how it is."

"I see *you*. Very charming, very foolish, very much a Monk. You can still walk away. Every woman here will know that you are right if you do."

The voices were raised again. He looked beyond the women. Otto had just driven up in a light truck. It had the identifying stencil of a *Lagerhaus*, a warehouse, on its side. His mother tried to take his arm when he stepped down from the driver's cabin but he shook her off. He met Konrad's eyes.

"I only have it for a half hour," he said.

"It's enough. It is wonderful that you have it. Help me with her." He bent over the woman. "Can you walk with help or shall we carry you?" he said.

She shook her head. "Not a German hospital, please."

He lifted her and carried her to the truck, aware of the murmuring voices of women. Otto lowered the tailboard and Konrad put the woman in the back of the truck. "I'll ride in here with her," he said.

"Do that."

Otto climbed behind the wheel. The truck started with a jerk then ran smoothly. Konrad could not see out of the vehicle. He was surprised when the truck stopped and Otto came around to the back. The woman seemed unconscious and she was limp when he lifted her out. He carried her into the house and he was aware of its limitations when he stood in the middle of the big room. He had not thought ahead. There was nowhere to lay her down except the floor. He eased her down gently then covered her with his second robe. He was not afraid of illness. Every Monk in the monastery had been a doctor of sorts. He had helped his share of them and he had had Father Stephen as his own patient ultimately. There was a variety of medicines in his cart, leftovers from his experience with Stephen; rough preparations, perhaps, and probably not approved by the medical fraternity, but remarkably effective.

"Are you certain that we can only have that truck for a half hour?" he said.

"Positive. And the man wants to be paid. I have no money but I had to take a chance. Is that all right? Can you do it? I told him we would."

There was worry in Otto's voice but there was a tone in that voice that Konrad had never heard before. Otto was talking to him as someone with whom he had shared an enterprise, a fellow adventurer who had gone against the will of women with him. It was vague, that impression, but he had it in his mind.

"How much?" he said.

Otto told him and he winced. It was exactly half of what he had received from the man for two days' work on the painting.

"I have it," he said. "Would he sell another half hour?"

"I don't know."

The woman was quiet under the robe. She could not be left for long and there was always the danger of intruders but some risk had to be taken.

"I'll ride with you," Konrad said. "We must have another half hour."

He climbed in beside the boy. "You surprised me when you brought this truck so fast."

"You expected me to bring it, didn't you?"

"I hoped that you would, yes."

"You didn't just hope. You told me to get it. Your voice sounded like you believed in me, like you trusted me to get it."

"I did."

"That never happened to me before."

"How did you get it?"

"I didn't know if I could." Otto stared ahead at the road. "I worked for Felix Wenzel last summer, some of the time lately after school. He owns the *Lagerhaus*. Sometimes I drove this. He knows me."

"I am grateful," Konrad said.

He was. He could see now what a position he would have held, in the middle of all those women, if Otto had not come back with a truck. Ultimately the police would have come, or someone would have called them, and the woman would have gone to a German hospital.

Otto pulled the car into an open space beside a long, flat-roofed building on the edge of the small residential section. Felix Wenzel came out when he heard the truck. Konrad introduced himself and drew his money from a hidden pocket.

"I just heard about that woman you hauled," the warehouse man said. "I didn't know about her when Otto asked for the truck. I hope she didn't have smallpox or something."

"She didn't. The truck is all right. I'd like another half hour."

Wenzel eyed the money in Konrad's hand. "Same rate," he said. "One half hour."

Otto had not spoken. He climbed behind the wheel. "It is too much," he said. "He does not pay the people working for him on the same basis."

"It makes no difference. I need his truck."

At his direction, Otto drove to the house of the man for whom he had restored the painting. The man was surprised but his eyes lighted when he saw Konrad.

"My friend!" he said. "You will never know."

"I am going to impose on you. My time is short. If you cannot help, do not hesitate to say so."

In short, clipped sentences Konrad told about the woman he had taken to his house. "I find that I will need things," he said. "I did not think about it. I need a mattress, a featherbed, anything she can rest on."

The man looked at him gravely. "You are foolhardy. You may make serious trouble for yourself. I would hate to see it. Yes. It did not occur to you, but I am a widower. I have a featherbed. It is extra. No one of mine needs it."

"I do not need a bed. Only a mattress. One of the feather mattresses would be wonderful."

"You may have it."

"And another thing." Konrad hesitated. "I apologize. I do not have time to shop. Do you have a bedpan?"

"I do. My wife was ill a long time. I may need it myself some day. Not now."

"I will borrow it. I will pay you for the mattress but later if you do not mind. I spent the money that you paid me to rent that truck outside."

"Do not worry. You need not pay me. The mattress is in the back room and it has something that you did not think about, a plastic cover, a protector. You are stronger than I."

Konrad hefted the mattress. It was heavy and awkward. He carried it to the truck and came back for the protector. The man had a bedpan in his hand, dusting it with a white cloth.

"Another thing," the man said, "I thought of it. Do you have a mop?"

The eyes of the two men met. It was another of the realities. Konrad shook his head and the man had the mop standing behind the door. "You may have it," he said.

There was nothing that one could say. Konrad shook hands with him and the man slapped his shoulder. "Good luck to you."

Otto was worried about time. It was a short distance to Konrad's place in the clearing but he hurried, obviously nervous. They stood together beside the truck when the mattress, the mop, and the bedpan had been unloaded.

"You are different than I thought," Otto said.

"You are different than I thought, too. We must know each other better."

"Maybe."

Otto turned abruptly and climbed into the truck. Konrad went into the house. There was still light but the dark would swiftly blot it out. It would not be easy to care for an ill patient in the darkness. He had a flashlight but it was a limited source of illumination.

The woman was lying where he had left her but she had rolled over on her back. She had been in distress during his absence and she had vomited. He was going to need the mop that the man had so thoughtfully provided.

The woman complained without opening her eyes when he lifted her from the floor but she sank gratefully into the featherbed. He swabbed the front of her dress. The damage there was slight. He would have to take his robe to the creek and wash it.

Monks had had illnesses like this in his time, a form of flu which attacked them when they were tired and cold, or when they had fasted too long. He took two tablets from his case, white tablets, and then one brown one. He regretted that he had no means of heating water. The woman struggled against taking the tablets but he succeeded in forcing them on her. She was not conscious. The fight in her was instinctive. He was beginning to see the enormity of the job ahead of him. This was not a Monk, this helpless patient in his care; this was a woman.

He walked out into his clearing and stood there, watching the light fade out of the sky above the trees. He remembered something that Father Stephen had told him long ago.

"Never speak to a woman after sunset," Father Stephen said.

The darkness dropped softly into the clearing.

Chapter Eight

The woman in the featherbed had two coughing attacks and another fit of nausea before she quieted down. She lay inert then, breathing heavily. Konrad went outside. There would be things to think about. This patient would need warm liquids, tea or soup mainly, and he had no way of heating anything. If he heated any liquid at a fire in the camping ground, it would lose its heat on the way back to this place where he lived.

The problem would wait until tomorrow because there was nothing that he could do about it tonight. He lifted his eyes to the stars. He needed help. He had, perhaps, acted recklessly but he could understand a foreign woman's fear of a German hospital. He could understand human fear, fear of anything. He had known fear. The woman had spoken to him in his native language. That had made her appeal a personal thing, addressed to him and to no one else.

He sat on the ground and turned his thought to God. He believed, as Father Stephen did, that words were unnecessary. It would be presumptuous and unreasonable to expect his Creator to listen patiently to words of his. He sat humbly in the awareness of God and his awareness was his prayer; whatever came to him in thought or memory was what God wanted him to dwell upon. There would be an answer to any problem if he listened quietly. He looked into the darkness at the far side of the clearing, the outer blank of darkness, and the day left him. He floated gently in the shapeless, colorless nothing that surrounded him, then came slowly to earth, to the awareness of a room and to voices speaking.

He was in the big room of the Czech farmer's house, the combination kitchen, bedroom, and parlor. The farmer and his wife slept there and all of the meals were eaten there. Father Stephen had slept there, too, while he was ill but he had been sleeping in the adjoining room now for months. He was well again, or as well as he would ever be. He looked old and thin and his magnificent beard was quite gray. His eyes looked disproportionately large in his thin face. They were intent eyes.

It was the fall of a year: 1961 probably. Konrad had done the work of two men on the farm through the long hot summer. He, too, was lean and hard and tired. The farmer had promised that, once the crops were in, he would help Stephen and himself to cross Czechoslovakia to Austria, using his connections with the underground. The crops were in.

"You have worked well," the farmer said. "You have been well fed and housed?"

"Yes."

"I would like you to work another year."

"No."

"You cannot leave without my help."

"You promised that help. It was our agreement."

"It might be that I could not keep the agreement as I planned. It might take another year."

"Then we would leave, Father Stephen and I. I would not work for you."

The farmer smiled. He was a man with no softness in him. "You would not survive a day if you left," he said. "You are refugees from Germany. The police would ask for papers and they would know that. They would send you back. A year with me would be easier."

Konrad looked into his eyes and read no yielding there. Father Stephen shifted in his chair. "My friend," he said. "The moment that Czechoslovakian police stopped us, and read our inadequate papers, we would tell them that we have been in their lovely country for six months. To their inevitable question we would answer by telling them that for those months we were shielded by your hospitality."

The farmer sat silent, staring at Stephen. He moved his hand on the tabletop, spreading the fingers and tightening them. "I cannot be at fault if I try to keep a good worker," he said. "If he will not stay I will help him to go."

He kept his word. There were way stations all across Czechoslovakia that were used by aliens, refugees, revolutionaries. It as a country ruled tyranically and seething with unrest. The farmer knew only the nearest members of the underground but each member knew someone else along the line. Most of the stations were farmhouses but there were places in the large cities, Prague and Brno. The members to whom they were referred knew the politics of their own area and they had almost infallible systems for avoiding police attention.

"It would cost you a large sum of money to travel so far in Czechoslovakia by the underground if you were not priests," the farmer said. "It is a very religious country and priests have not done well. They will ask little of you."

They had given what they had in skill and in a feeling for people, he and Stephen. It had been a slow journey, a matter of moving at the right time, often a matter of passing a certain place when a certain man was on duty. The journey was mainly in winter weather, in cold and in heavy snow. Stephen did not complain but he lacked the strength to endure long hours on the road.

They reached Vienna in the week before Christmas. To Konrad it was the most beautiful city he had ever seen and it was good to have the furtive life of the underground behind him. Austria was neither shocked nor startled by refugees. A poor country in world's goods, a country of low wages, it had been host to more refugees than any other country except West Germany. Konrad and Father Stephen established identity in Austria and they were accepted for what they were. The Christmas of their faith came later than the Christmas of the Romans so they attended High Mass in St. Stephen's Cathedral on Christmas Day.

There was a sculptured figure in the cathedral, Anton Pilgram's sculpture of himself, that fascinated Konrad. He returned many times to visit it. The lean-faced figure looked remarkably like Konrad, particularly in profile. The cheekbones were high, the nose straight, the chin thrusting. There were brackets, too, that swept from the nose corner around the ends of a rather wide mouth. He called the image to Stephen's attention on their second visit to the cathedral, one of the few they made together. Stephen dismissed his idea impatiently.

"An older man, that," he said. "Much more worldly. I see no resemblance whatever."

The problem in Vienna was the simple problem of eating. There were minor problems such as a place in which to live and clothing to replace those articles of apparel that were ragged and torn, but the desperate problem was food.

Stephen was sixty-three and he had come through a severe illness. He coughed a lot and he had little stamina for sustained effort of any kind. He had no small skills and his experience with human beings and human affairs had been the experience of a religious. As a religious he was on strange ground, too. He rejected any suggestion that they contact Russian Orthodox priests in Vienna.

"We do not know who they are," he said.

Father Basil at the monastery had deplored Father Stephen's withdrawal from all churches and churchmen who had bowed to the decrees of Moscow.

"They have saved what they could," he said. "Some of them have not been honest, some have been indecently ambitious, but many still serve God. We all survive as men of prayer because we made compromises. God will judge if the compromises were wicked. Do not set up a religion of your own in your heart, Stephen. It is not enough."

"I hold in my heart only the religion of my lifetime," Stephen said. "It *is* enough."

Konrad had reached an understanding of Basil's point over the years. He believed that they should have friendly relations with the Russian priests who had churches in the cities that they visited, some of whom were certainly in exile for the same reason as Stephen. In the end, however, he followed Stephen's code rather than Basil's. There was one great fact that, to him, sustained Stephen's position and justified it.

God was never closer to him, never more real, than when Stephen spoke of God, or when he remembered Stephen speaking of God.

They had only a small remnant of money when they reached Vienna. They rented a small flat on the third floor of a very old walkup apartment not far from St. Stephen's Cathedral, an apartment building like the one Mozart had lived in, with a musician's court on the ground floor and banistered walkarounds on each floor above it. It was a difficult climb for Father Stephen, insuring the fact that he would go out seldom, but it was the best that they could do and they paid half of the rent with promises. That left the problem of food.

It was Konrad's responsibility to earn money since Stephen could not, and Konrad's task to find food.

Konrad, that winter, was seventeen years old.

It was logical to seek first in the museums for employment. The first man to whom he was referred had no interest in a Russian and was contemptuous of monastery experience without testing monastery skill.

Konrad was self-conscious about his speech. The German that he had learned in the monastery was Prussian German. The Austrians spoke like Bavarians and Prussian was harsh to them. Listening to them, Konrad found Prussian harsh, too.

He walked a great many miles on strange streets and he tried several museums before he found an antique dealer who was willing to give him an opportunity to prove what he could do.

"I would like a piece of work for which I can be paid quickly," Konrad said. "There are two of us and we have no money."

The dealer was a slight, short man with a clipped mustache and a high bald forehead. He had cold gray eyes.

"An easy job?" he said.

"No. A difficult one."

"Why?"

"I'd enjoy it more and earn more money."

The dealer grunted and led Konrad down a steep narrow staircase to a basement. There was a door then and a deeper basement. They entered a room of wood carvings, some the height of a living person, some that could be held in a man's hand. The dealer took an image from the great mantel. It was fifteen inches tall and, oddly, the carving of a Monk.

"What kind of wood is that?" he said.

"Ash."

Konrad, who could not have named the tree if he saw it, could name the wood. He turned the figure around in his hand. It was dirty, with the dirt clinging to it in crusts, and it was smoke-blackened. There were spots that looked like damage from insects.

"What would you do if I asked you to restore that?"

"I'd wash it to see what it looked like, then I'd probably soak it in hot paraffin wax. That might be enough, but I could repair it if I had to do so."

"How?"

"I'd carve what I needed and put it in place with a good glue. You'd never know."

"You could do this?"

"Yes."

"I believe you."

"I would, of course, need tools. A wood carver needs special tools."

"I know. Come here."

In another room there was a bench with clamps and a vise. Konrad opened drawers. There was a variety of clamps and gouges, a variety of stones and straps, a mallet. There were fluters, gauges, chisels, rifflers, sand paper, the whole kit.

"This is fine," he said.

"A carver worked here. He was pretty good. I'll tell you what I'll do. I'll try you for a week and I'll pay you in advance since you need money. If I keep you on, we'll forget the advance unless you quit. If you quit me, I'll collect."

Konrad thought of what a week's wages would mean if he got those wages immediately. The salary sounded low but he could make it do. "Thank you," he said. "I'll work for you."

He worked in that subbasement for a long time. He reported in the morning and descended to his working space. Usually he did not see any one all day unless he had a new job or a completed job to discuss with Mr. Zicker, the proprietor. He worked steadily through the carvings and when Mr. Zicker discovered that he could handle cracked or broken porcelain he added another department to his work.

He had little personal life. Father Stephen was alone all day and eager for talk at night. They had a small stove and once they were established, with pots and pans and a few dishes of their own, Stephen did most of the cooking. Konrad protested his taking on that chore.

"It is beneath your dignity," he said.

"A man adds to his dignity with each new task that he learns to do," Father Stephen said.

In time Konrad bought a radio, a small but powerful set which brought in programs of Russian, German, Czech, Italian, English; sometimes Romanian or Bulgarian. Father Stephen delighted in it, and they listened to it together in the evening but Father Stephen wanted news of the day, details of what was happening in the streets, what people talked about. Konrad, in his isolation, knew nothing of what was happening in Vienna so he added an hour to his day and walked the streets, initially at random and ultimately on a pattern.

There was the Danube River and its bridges and there were Roman ruins, incredibly old churches, old mansions, in unexpected places. There was a tavern called The Twelve Apostles and there were libraries, museums, parks. Konrad took Vienna into his mind, memorizing it. Ultimately Father Stephen, who rarely descended the stairs, insisted that Konrad take one night a week out. Konrad listened to music then, the many varieties of music that made up the sound of Vienna, and he tried the beer halls where a man could sit and sing all night with one stein of beer. He cleaned a painting for Mr. Zicker, something completely out of his regular line of work at the shop, and the proprietor took him to dinner. It was a restaurant with music and a small stage. There, for the first time in his life, Konrad fell in love.

Her name was Deslys, or the restaurant said that it was. She was small and blonde and very simply dressed, with none of the glamour or glitter that Konrad associated with actresses and entertainers. She came out on the stage, smiling, acting delighted that she was where she was, a friendly girl. He liked the way she moved, the graceful gestures of her hands. She sang.

She did not sing very well. Her voice was untrained, but she sang like a girl having a good time. Some of her songs had lyrics that shocked Konrad but she sang them simply and Konrad, looking at her, could not associate evil with her.

He could never remember what Mr. Zicker talked about that night, nor what they ate. He remembered only that Mr. Zicker paid little attention to Deslys and that he did not seem impressed with her. He could not understand that at all.

He lay awake that night remembering her. He and Stephen had two narrow beds, one on each side of the room with a table and two chairs in between. He could hear Stephen's heavy breathing, almost a snoring, and the eyes of his mind saw Deslys.

If he had had the money, he would have dined every night in the restaurant where she sang. He walked over there several nights, hoping that he would see her going in or coming out. He could not imagine speaking to her; it would be enough to see her. He never did. He liked, however, the sign outside the place where she was. It read:

Deslys
The Vesper Trio

He saved his money for a week and went back to the restaurant alone. Without Mr. Zicker he was unimpressive, and he was poorly dressed. He was given a badly situated table at the rear. Waiters and customers passed back and forth between him and the stage. He could not see Deslys clearly but he could see her. She moved around the stage brightly and happily and he felt again that this was a girl who loved life. His own life was brighter and happier seeing her and hearing her, even from a distance.

He saved his money for another week, cutting down on every non-essential thing, even to the meat in his luncheon sandwiches. He went back to the restaurant and stopped, staring at the sign. It read:

Katinka
The Vesper Trio

Deslys was gone. Someone else was singing and dancing where she had sung and danced. He was in awe of the waiters in the restaurant and he could not have asked one of them where she was. It would make no difference. He could not follow if he knew. He turned and walked down the street with the feeling that he was leaving something important behind him.

He never did recover entirely from Deslys. She came back to him in dreams and in the odd corners of his thinking.

Vienna, of course, had made him aware of women. They were everywhere. In the growing years of his life there had been no women. There had been no women within his range of vision in Dresden and only the aging wife of the farmer on the farm in Czechoslovakia. He walked streets in Vienna that were rainbows of women. He liked the lightness and the grace of them, their manner of holding heads on one side, looking out of the corners of their eyes. He liked the mystery and the strangeness of them and they excited him vaguely but he did not know any of them and his work, two stories underground, did not bring him in contact with women. No one of them commanded a place in his memory. Deslys alone dwelt there.

Another man came to work in the space next door to Konrad's. He was a fairly young man, in his thirties, a loose-lipped man with a drooping lid on his left eye and little color in his skin. He was a specialist in worked metal: bronze, copper, steel, zinc, and silver. Mr. Zicker had given him a large stack of jewelry to repair, restore, or recombine. He came into Konrad's room on his first day.

"So you're Zicker's mystery expert?" he said. "It is worth working in this dump awhile just to see you. People talk about you and nobody has seen you."

"I don't know why anyone would talk about me."

"Don't you? Well, it's not easy to keep secrets in the antique business. You're the fellow who did that batch of wood carvings, aren't you?"

"I didn't do them. I cleaned them up."

"Plus and plus and plus. That's one of the best lots of wood out of here in years. Zicker sent the lot to England, probably for the U.S."

"I didn't know."

"Well, get wise."

The man's name was Lou Erlander. He had surly mornings when he made no effort to be friendly but there were other times when he was an interesting companion. He had a skill close to genius in a field that was new at that time to Konrad. He could fashion earrings and pendants and pins out of boxes of junk, working sometimes with incredible speed.

"I've got a better thing, too, that I do," he said. "I can make replicas of mosaic murals, the old ones. I won't let you see me do it and I won't do it for Zicker, but it's a thing I've got."

He was a strange individual. Konrad went out with him one evening and they sat for hours in a beer hall. Erlander drank an enormous amount of beer but he did not get sodden with it. The singing seemed to amuse him but he did not join in with it. He was a chain smoker.

At that period Konrad was enjoying a spell of freedom from responsibility in his evenings. There was an elderly Pole named Josef who heard Konrad and Stephen speaking Russian one night and who came in to join them. He and Stephen visited in the daylight hours while Konrad was away and they often extended their sessions into the evenings. They listened to the radio together and they discussed the news and they played checkers.

Lou Erlander was the first friend that Konrad had ever had. There were, of course, the Monks, and many of them close to his heart, but they were comrades, companions of the monastery, not friends in the usual sense of the word.

Lou Erlander belonged in his world, a man of artistic skills and artistic tastes and little money. Erlander showed him sides of Vienna that he would never have discovered by himself.

They were seated one night in a semi-basement cafe, below street level but open to the sky, a place with space between tables and a restless patronage that moved back and forth in that space. Prostitutes, singly or in pairs, hesitated before passing or, more boldly, tried to join them at the table. Lou Erlander wasted no time on them. He had one phrase and he used it on any would-be sitter.

"Keep walking," he said.

Konrad wondered about those girls. Some of them seemed too young to be what he knew them to be. Invariably they wore dark shadow on their eyes, black lines on their eyelashes. He had learned to associate eye make-up with prostitutes on the basis of a very limited observation of women and Deslys was brighter in his memory as the result. Deslys had been blonde, light in her coloring, with blue eyes. Thinking of her, he had been watching one of the girls. He came back to his table suddenly, aware that Lou Erlander was watching him.

"How old are you, Kon?" Lou said.

"Nearly twenty."

Lou shook his head. "You look older than that and yet not so old. Ever had a woman, Kon?"

"No."

"I thought not. You aren't queer, are you?"

"What do you mean?"

"You don't go for men do you, or want them going for you?"

"No. Oh, no. Certainly not."

The idea shook him. He had not known about homosexuality until he came to Vienna and he knew very little about it when he did learn that there was such a thing. Lou was watching him. His damaged left eye gave his face a villainous quality when he concentrated.

"You're moving into it in one form or another," he said. "It's none of my business but you're somebody who can be hurt, really hurt. How have you managed to keep out of it this long? In Vienna, of all places! No men, no women . . ."

"I'm a Monk," Konrad said.

"A what?"

Konrad tried to explain. He told Lou Erlander about the monastery and Father Stephen. Lou whistled softly.

"That's the Goddamnedest," he said. "And you're supporting a priest? Saying prayers every night."

"Yes."

"And you're a Monk. Well, I've seen all there is to see. Konrad, without knowing, or wanting to know, how much you draw in salary from that obscenely smiling crocodile, Zicker, I'll tell you what to do. Walk out on him and go to work for someone else for twice as much."

"I didn't get twice as much, or anything at all, until I came here."

"You would now. You and the priest would eat better."

"We eat all right."

"Good for you. Anyway I told you. I could set you up for one of these whores. It might be good for you, maybe not. Sometimes I think I know things that I don't, but like I told you, you're moving into it one of these days; all the bright little green, yellow, and red fireworks of sex. Make it with a woman, Kon, and not just one of these tramps. A young guy who looks the way you do can make it where you'd least expect."

That was his last night with Lou Erlander. Two days later Lou moved on to someplace else without a good-bye. He did not report for work in the morning; he was just gone. It was like Deslys, or a little like Deslys.

Konrad walked into Zicker's office the day after Lou disappeared and demanded a raise. He was friendly and firm and he got it. The incident had meaning for him beyond the money involved, meaning that he felt and that he did not try to define. He felt older, more mature, taller in the place where he stood.

Father Stephen lasted five years. He died quietly one night in his sleep, taking the last step with the same quiet dignity that had stamped his life.

Konrad did not try to stay in Vienna after Stephen was gone. He walked away from the city, literally walked. He walked long roads and saw vast mountains on his horizons. He walked beside rivers and he camped in forests. He turned corners and saw church spires against the sky and when they were onion-shaped towers he liked them better. He bought a cart that was designed to carry boats over portages and he collected a miscellany of tools and glues and varnishes, waxes and resins and odd chemical substances. He stopped at strange doors and offered to fix broken things of sentimental value. He talked to many people and he discovered that most of them were as lonely as he was. Ultimately because Munich was a city named with the word that was German for "Monks," he wanted to see Munich.

He finished his prayer hour, sitting on the ground in Munich with his back to the wall of the shack in which he lived, a shack that had once been a place of sin. There had been many pictures in his mind and he rose slowly.

He had made his prayer and he had asked for answers. There was a woman in his house. She was not an attractive woman. She was ill. She had said that she was afraid of a German hospital and that was, no doubt, true. She had said that she was Russian and she was not. He had known that when he heard her speak. He had owed her nothing and he had brought her here. She was a situation in his life.

He knew what Father Stephen would tell him to do. He could call forth the words. He knew what Lou Erlander would say, could almost hear him speak. He had asked for an answer and he had answers.

He stood before his house and he let the voices fade as the pictures had faded. He opened his door and walked into his house. All that he could remember was that someone who was alone had asked him for help.

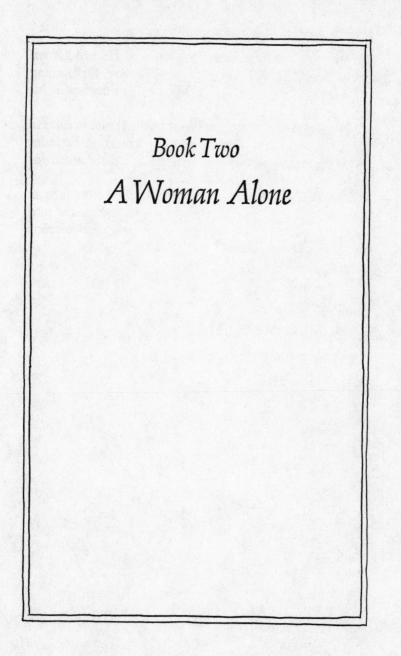

Book Two

A Woman Alone

Chapter One

The woman moaned. She turned on her side, uttered a protesting sound and rolled into the depths of the feather-bed, lying on her back again. She did not open her eyes. She seemed to be crying. She struggled to rise then fell back, her right arm across her eyes.

Konrad stood inside the door, watching her. It was early morning and pale light flowed into the room. There were realities with which he had to cope and they could, he knew, defeat him. He had to provide nourishment for this woman and it had to be hot. A soup would be perfect. He had no means of making soup, no means of heating anything, but if he could not feed the woman, he would have to surrender her to someone who could feed her.

The other problem was almost as grave. If this were a Monk, this patient in the bed, he would strip him and bathe him, rectify the accidents of illness and unconsciousness, make him physically comfortable. This was a woman. Something in his mind corrected him and said, "This is a human being, neither man nor woman, a creature who is ill." He still could not do for her what he would do for a Monk.

He knelt beside her and prayed. He said his morning

prayers and a special prayer for her. He had given her to the night with prayer, certain in his soul that she would be safe until morning, but he did not overreach. He knew how to pray. He could not draw upon faith to carry her through the day as it had carried her through the night. He prayed for strength and for wisdom to do what was right for her, accepting in his own person full responsibility for whatever must be done.

He wanted to move her out of the bed and wash the protective cover but he had no place to put her except the floor. He shook his head. He would be doing at best a partial job and disturbing her out of proportion to the value of it.

A voice hailed him from the clearing. Otto was standing a few feet from the door. He had a package in his hand.

"How is she?" he said.

"About the same; no better, no worse."

"I came early. I have to get to school. I brought her some soup in a Thermos."

"Soup?"

"Yes. My mother said she would need it."

"Did your mother send it?"

"In a way, she did. I talked to her."

Konrad stretched out his hand. He would not have dared to hope for this, nor have imagined receiving it. "You have no idea what this means, Otto," he said.

"It's chicken soup. We had some for supper last night. This was left. I've got to go."

He turned and hurried across the clearing. Konrad walked into the house. In the brown paper sack with the Thermos bottle there was a cup and a spoon. He poured some of the soup and tasted it. It was hot, not too hot, easy to swallow. He knelt beside the woman and shook her.

He shook her three times before her eyes opened. She looked dazed.

"You must take this," he said.

He lifted her head, one hand behind her neck and fed one spoonful of soup to her. She swallowed and blinked.

"Hospital?" she said. "No."

"No. It is my place."

They spoke in Russian. She either remembered to do that or there was some subconscious guardian cautioning her. He fed her another spoonful of soup and another. She swallowed mechanically. She blinked and kept blinking. She had almost finished the cup of soup when she sat straight, away from his supporting hand. She looked around the room then down at herself. She made a moaning sound and lifted one hand before her face.

"Get out of here!" she said. "Go away from me."

"But—"

"Get out!"

She hiccoughed and bent over, her face in her hands. She was weak, of course, and there was shock in her. Konrad could understand the shock. He did not believe that she would be strong enough to do what she would want to do, but he could not help her; she would not permit that. He backed slowly to the door.

The police car rolled to the clearing edge as he stepped out. The two policemen walked toward him. They were not hurrying but there was determination in them, or sense of purpose. They omitted the customary friendly greetings.

"You know better than to bring a woman to this place," the elder policeman said.

"She was ill."

"None of your concern. There are hospitals for that."

"She spoke to me in Russian. She was afraid of German hospitals."

"We have better hospitals than the Russians."

"She isn't Russian."

"What is she?"

"I'd guess Czech."

"We have to see her."

"She won't want it. She was unconscious for quite a while. No woman around. She is embarrassed."

The older policeman went inside and the woman's voice rose high to protest. "Get out!" she said. "Get out!"

The policeman retreated. "I was prepared to take her to the hospital," he said. "She is not exactly helpless. I can respect a woman's privacy to a point." He rubbed the back of his neck with his right hand. "You cannot, of course, keep her here and we have to know who she is."

The younger policeman, as he usually did, remained silent while the older man was taking the lead. He came in now.

"We could probably set a time limit," he said, "and let the Monk get the woman ready. After all, he brought her here and she can't run away."

The older man nodded. "How about it? Will two hours be enough?"

"For me. Probably not for her. Will you consider something?"

"What?"

"I don't know any more about her than you do. She is a woman alone. She had one friend here, somebody who moved to Frankfurt. She probably doesn't have very good papers. People like this woman do not come into West Germany unless they are trying to get away from Communist governments."

He could read understanding in the policeman's eyes, a

measure of sympathy. This was a familiar problem. West Germany had been inundated at one time by the tide of people, millions, who had been expelled from lands and cities taken over by Poland, Russia, and Czechoslovakia. Those refugees had been Germans, and the West Germans handled them so well that countless refugees of foreign origin had followed them into the country.

"She cannot stay here. You know that," the policeman said. "We strained a point to permit *you* to stay. But a woman?"

"She is recovering from her illness. She was unconscious yesterday. A little more time! She may remember friends, do something about her own problem."

"A little more time, where? Here? No stove for hot food, no decent facilities of any kind. No woman around."

The policeman shook his head. "No. We cannot have it. The only answer is a hospital."

"She is terrified of hospitals."

"And Germans."

"Not necessarily. It is the hospital that frightens her. I am a Monk. I could take care of her. A hospital would demand of her information that she does not want to give, information that it might be dangerous for her to give."

He touched a sensitive nerve there. The two policemen exchanged glances. In Germany many doubtful facts were accepted, many flaws in papers overlooked, in preference to expelling a person whose enforced return to a Communist country would be a doom, a sentence to death or imprisonment for political sin.

"Let us give them the day to work it out," the younger policeman said.

"The day? Yes. We could do that. Till 4 P.M. But the woman cannot spend another night here."

"Thank you," Konrad said.

He had no solution to the problem in his mind, no possible solution, no answer that would ring true at 4 P.M. and not be operative now. He took time gratefully, however, and did not question the hours ahead. He would face those hours inevitably in their time.

The two policemen turned away and walked across the clearing, the younger man in the lead. The older man was frowning, obviously not in approval of the compromise, even while making it. He had offered two hours and he had ended by giving most of the day.

The clearing was quiet after the police Volkswagen left. Konrad turned back to the house, hesitated, and then opened the door quietly. The woman was sitting in the center of the room, her head resting on her forearms, her arms across her knees. She was wearing his second robe, engulfed in it, and her own clothing was rolled into a small bundle, pushed into a corner of the room. She had made some effort to clean the place and the effort had obviously been too much for her. She was crying softly.

"Will you take a little more of the soup?" Konrad said.

Her head came up swiftly. She made a hurried, grabbing motion to the front of the robe. "Go away from me!" she said. "Stay away! Go!"

He stood his ground unhappily. "I would like to do something for you, help you in some way."

"Just go! I hate you. I hate the sight of you."

"I will go. I have to leave for a little while. Take some of the soup. You need it."

He closed the door and walked away from it. He was disconcerted. He knew of no reason why the woman should hate him. He had tried to serve her since she first appealed to him for help. He shook his head. He could understand her disliking his appearance. He remembered commenting on it once, only once, to Father Stephen. It was after they had seen and discussed the Anton Pilgram self-sculpture in the cathedral.

"I am ill-favored in appearance," he said then. "I would never have been accepted as an apostle."

They were standing before the high altar. Father Stephen was gazing upward at the painting of *The Stoning of Saint Stephen.* His eyes were narrowed.

"The apostles, I imagine, were extraordinarily ugly men," he said. "It is of no importance. The shape of your face is a minor matter. Concern yourself with the shape of your soul."

Konrad did not, he was certain, concern himself unduly with the shape of his face but when his appearance was called to his attention he thought of himself as one of the "extraordinarily ugly men." He was, he thought gloomily, undoubtedly unpleasing to the eye of a woman but he did not understand why this one should hate him.

He walked to the bathhouse. He needed its facilities since those at home were denied to him. A cold shower made him feel more cheerful and he bought a quart of milk on the way home. It was the only portable food that he could think of and the woman undoubtedly needed food. Thinking of that made him realize more fully that he had been an utter fool in taking on a responsibility for which he was unequipped. Realizing that, he still believed that he would make the same decision under the same circumstances if the decision were his to make again.

There is little real logic in me, he thought.

He knocked at the door before pushing it open gently. The woman rolled off the corner of the featherbed where she had been lying. She drew his robe around her as she rolled and sat up. She was dark-haired, dark-eyed, with a thin face, a hostile woman and unpleasant in appearance.

"I brought you milk," he said. "I am sorry I cannot provide better."

"That is fine. Thank you. Put it on the floor near the door."

"I could bring it over to you."

"No." Her body straightened. "Don't come in here. Get out of here."

He backed away from the savagely thrown words and put the milk down on the floor. He was closing the door again from the outside when he heard her voice.

"No! Come back here," she said. "I want to talk to you."

He stepped into the room, only to have her voice stop him again inside the door. She was still sitting on the floor.

"There is no bath here," she said. "No place to take a bath."

"No. I'm sorry. There is a bathhouse. I go there. It is nearly a mile."

"I will have to go."

"You are not strong enough."

"I will make myself strong enough."

He stared at her, surprised at the sudden discovery that she was a young woman. She had existed for him until this moment without any age. She closed one hand into a small fist, then opened it again.

"I have no clothes," she said. "You must get them for me."

"I?"

"Yes. *My* clothes. My own clothes. They are downtown. In two bags. In a hotel. I must have them."

"I cannot. I do not know downtown or hotels or women's clothes. It is impossible."

Her eyes were steady on his. "It is not impossible," she said. "The impossibility is that I can get them myself." She gestured to the robe in which she was wrapped. "Or that I can go to a bathhouse! Or that I can sit here forever like this! To make things possible I must have my clothes. You must get them for me. I have no one else."

"You said that you hated me."

"I do. I have never hated anyone more. But I must have my clothes. Come back in ten minutes and I will have the money and the instructions."

He stood, looking at her, resenting her assumption of authority, resenting everything about her, and he was aware of minutes ticking away, of policemen scheduled to return at the end of a grace period. He was aware, too, with a sense of shock, that the girl was holding herself erect with an effort, that her face was white.

"I'll come back," he said gruffly.

It was a sunny afternoon out of doors. There was a nameless bird singing, a bird with a contralto voice. Konrad walked the length of the clearing and back. He could not imagine going to a hotel and asking for a woman's clothes, if that was what she required of him. There were things that a man could do and things that could only be listed among impossibilities, feats that he should not be called upon to attempt.

The voice of Father Stephen came to him across the years as it often did. He had been in despair one day at the monastery over a task given to him by an elderly irascible Monk.

"There are impossibilities in your mind that are not impossibilities in the small world of your living," Father Stephen said. "Before you reject a task as impossible, ask yourself why God presented you with this thing to be done."

He asked himself the question now and he had no answer. He made a one-eighty turn at the house and started again down the length of the clearing. Werner stepped through the green screen and waved his hand.

"How is your patient?" he said.

"Improving, I believe. I missed you yesterday."

"Sorry I wasn't around. I hear that Otto did a star turn for you."

"I could not have made out if Otto had not been there. Today is your turn."

"Doing what?"

"Finding a hotel downtown."

"I don't know much about downtown. That's a fact. What hotel?"

"I'll tell you in a minute."

Konrad crossed the clearing to the house and knocked at the door, astonished that he was knocking. He opened the door then and there was an envelope on the floor. The girl was probably in one of the other rooms. He stood where he was and opened the envelope.

There was no salutation. *I have two bags at the Hotel Bayerischer Hof, Promenadeplatz 6,* she wrote. *Ask for the porter. The hotel is keeping the bags for me. There is no charge but give the porter twenty marks. If you have any trouble give him the enclosed note. Please buy me another quart Thermos bottle and have it filled with soup at the hotel grillroom. I like their soup.*

> *Thank you,*
> *Ursula Vaclav*

There were fifty marks in a small envelope. Konrad read the note again and the shorter note addressed to the hotel, requesting that her bags be delivered to bearer. The handwriting was clear, clean, and she wrote in German. It was interesting that she did not write in Russian. One would find it easier, of course, to speak Russian than to read or write it. He read her name again, pronouncing it, Ursula Vaclav.

He had an impulse to call out, to let her know, in whatever room she was, that he had read her note and that he would do the best he could. There did not seem to be much sense in telling her that, so he let the impulse die. He walked out to the clearing where Werner waited for him.

"Do you know how to find the Hotel Bayerischer Hof?" he said.

"I think so. I've never been there."

"Look."

Konrad handed him the note. Werner read it and whistled softly. "If she stayed there, she's rich," he said. "Nobody stays there but wealthy foreigners."

"I don't believe so. I do not believe she is wealthy, I mean."

"She has to be."

"Anyway, we have to go there. How do we go?"

"We? I didn't say I was going."

"I need help. I cannot do it alone."

Werner looked toward the house, frowning slightly. "That's funny, me helping you," he said slowly. "I never figured on its working out that way. I was going to punch your face in. I didn't like you. I don't like people who come in giving orders like you did. I don't like rich people, either. Somehow, it is easy to like you. You are different. You fascinate me."

"Thanks. I liked you that first day. I told you so."

"Yes. That didn't make sense either. All right. I'll help you but you'll have to pay my carfare. We take a number eight trolley. You know where it runs, between here and the bathhouse."

"I know."

They walked to the waiting platform where the trolley stopped. Werner asked the motorman of the streetcar about the Bayerischer Hof. He had an odd assurance, Werner, a slightly aggressive assurance. He did not talk much as the trolley made its way downtown. Like Konrad he was obviously having an unusual experience. His assurance returned to him when the trolley reached the Karlsplatz, a terminal point that was jammed with traffic, blue and white streetcars, red buses, and all manner and color of automobiles.

"It is near here," he said.

They found Promenadeplatz and walked it, a wide street with a dividing line of parkway between its two automobile lanes, a parkway of trees, flowers, and monuments. The Bayerischer Hof was a long gray stone building with awninged shops on its street front and an obvious roof garden topping it. Konrad stared at it silently. There were cars and taxi cabs pulling up to its entrance or moving away, well-dressed people entering it or leaving it. His confidence, never very strong, faded. He shook his head.

"We must first buy the Thermos bottle," he said.

They bought the Thermos bottle in a shop only two blocks away and walked slowly back, walking the sidewalk that ran in front of the hotel. Konrad looked across the wide promenade at the two belfries of the Frauenkirche, dull red in color and tipped with green-capped towers. This was the distinctive symbol of Munich which he had seen often in pictures. It did not seem real, seen in actuality. This whole experience, for that matter, was steeped in unreality. He would not have chosen to be here, to do what he was committed to do. He turned slowly, reluctantly, to the hotel entrance.

He was seldom conscious of his appearance but he was aware of it now. He was not wearing his robe. He wore only the attire of a laborer, shapeless, stained trousers, a gray shirt that had seen long wear, a brown sweater. Werner looked little better. He had an old gray jacket, a blue shirt without a necktie, brown slacks. The lobby was a pattern of people, attractively dressed men and women. There was a long counter to the left of the door, elevators facing it. Konrad moved to the right and was rewarded when he saw the grillroom sign.

"We will buy the soup," he said.

He was evading, and knew that he was evading, the ordeal of asking for the girl's luggage. He was aware, too, of Werner's silence. Werner did not feel confident or at home in this place, either. That thought restored his command of himself. There was a waiter, or a captain of waiters, who looked at him inquiringly.

"I would like a quart of your soup in the Thermos bottle," he said.

"Certainly."

He hesitated then. "And may we have soup, too, eating it here?"

Momentarily his hesitation was contagious, then the waiter said "Certainly" again and led them to a corner table, masked in shadow. It was an off-hour and there were few people in the grillroom.

"I am hungry," Werner said.

"I am, too. I did not know it until we came in here."

"Your woman is rich. She must be. She lived here."

"She is not my woman. I know nothing about her."

The waiter brought soup and large rolls with butter. Konrad ate gratefully, liking the Bayerischer Hof for providing such food. When he entered the lobby again with Werner he was no longer overawed. He sought the porter and presented the note which the girl had written. The porter read, raised his eyebrows and nodded.

"Ah, yes. Miss Vaclav. We have kept her bags safely for her."

It took only five minutes to accept two surprisingly heavy bags, sign for them, give the porter twenty marks and leave the hotel. It was still a bright day and in the distance Konrad could see a high slender-shaped tower which seemed to be supporting two flying saucers.

"There is a restaurant on top of that," Werner said, "and you can see all of Munich while you dine. I have never been there."

"I will not be there either."

"I worked last summer near it. On Rubble Hill."

"Rubble Hill?"

"Yes, some people called it Trash Hill. All that place out there is where the Olympic Games will be in 1972. My father helped to make the hill. My mother did too, a little."

"How?"

"I'll tell you. It's a long story. On the trolley."

"And you worked there? I didn't know you worked."

"I know. It's the way I talk. We are poor people. In summer out of school I have to work."

"Why aren't you proud of it?"

"Because it's meaningless."

"I don't believe so."

"I do."

They boarded a number eight trolley, waiting for them at Karlsplatz. A sign on the car read HASENBERGL. Konrad settled into his seat.

"All right," he said. "You are not proud of working when you could be loafing, of earning money when your family needs money. You say that all of that is meaningless. Tell me about Rubble Hill."

"You don't understand a damned thing. I tried to tell you something."

"What?"

"Never mind. About Rubble Hill. That has meaning. You won't understand that, either. Munich was bombed in the war. It was all smashed. I wasn't born yet, so I never saw that. For a long time nobody in Munich could do anything about fixing it. Everybody was busy trying to make a living. My father says they were very hard times. Anyway, the men of Munich, my father and other men, wanted their city to look beautiful again like they remembered it, so when they finished work on their jobs every day, they gave a few hours to cleaning up rubble and wrecked places and hauling stuff. There was a place where they could take the stuff, all the bricks and stone and wrecked furniture and bones, everything, and in a few years they made a big hill."

"What did you do out there?"

"Not much. It was all finished. When they had all the rubbish out there, they brought in soil from the country and covered the hill, then they planted grass on the soil and put in young trees. They made three hills, actually, a big one and two small ones. It is all a park. I watered grass and helped the tree men. It was a good job, I guess, better than most."

"And, still, you weren't proud of it?"

"I told you, you don't understand."

Konrad stared out of the window. The story of Rubble Hill, as Werner told it, was a simple story but it had not been a simple story, of course, for the men who had written it with their toil. One could not imagine the lives that other people lived: one had to hear about them. Life demanded different things from different people. Why? Maybe Werner was correct. He was without understanding.

"Some men march," Father Stephen said once, "and

some men make the music for the marching, and other men direct them where to go. A parade is a simple thing and could hardly be simpler, but it uses people in different ways as life does."

The trolley stopped at the platform near the bathhouse. Werner carried one of the bags and Konrad, who also carried the soup, carried the other. He looked toward the trees, the forest where he lived. He had the bags and possessions of Ursula Vaclav and he was a little late. The police, he thought, would be there before him and he had no answer for them.

Chapter Two

There was a stranger in the clearing, a man in post office uniform, when Konrad returned with the bags. Werner had left him where the path turned in from the road, so he was carrying the two bags and the Thermos bottle. The stranger looked at him, his eyebrows raised.

"Need help?" he said.

"No thanks. I will be out in a minute if you want me."

"Carry on."

The man resumed his pacing. Konrad knocked at the door, then entered without waiting for permission. There was no one visible within but the girl came from an inner room when he thumped the bags down noisily on the floor. She was drawing his robe tightly about her.

"You got them?" she said. "I'm glad." Then, in the same breath, she said: "Who is that man outside?"

"I don't know. I'll find out."

He returned to the clearing and the man walked toward him. "You are the Monk, Konrad?" he said.

"Yes."

"I am Kurt Ziegler. I am the brother of a policeman who is much interested in you."

"There are two."

"My brother, Bruno, is the younger one. He told me about your predicament."

"Did he? I am sorry that I cannot invite you into the house. I can only offer grass to sit on."

"The lady in the house is clamourously unfriendly. I tried entering the house. Your grass will be fine. As you will have noticed I am a carrier of mail. We carriers have little experience in sitting. We sit gratefully anywhere."

The man was young, probably about his own age, Konrad thought, and about the same general build, a man with humor in his eyes and a pleasant curve to his mouth. He lighted a cigarette when he seated himself.

"It is this way," he said. "Bruno is impressed with you and he doesn't believe that you will handle the young woman in there without help. He doesn't believe that you will get a woman to help you, either." He smiled and made a half-gesture with his right hand. "Germany has too many women as it is, a condition which makes women dissatisfied with one another. There is little enthusiasm on the part of women for female refugees; none at all for female Russians."

"Your brother and his partner have ordered me out of here before nightfall."

"And you haven't a place to go?"

"Frankly, no."

"Have you ever heard of Streber Gardens?"

"No."

"It is an old German idea. It has been working in German cities since 1900. If a man is in a low-income group and lives in the city, with no land, no place where he can put his hands in the soil, he pays 100 marks a year ($25.00) and he is given a plot of ground on which he can build a house, a shed, a shack, a place to which he can go on his day off, or weekends, and grow flowers or vegetables or whatever he wishes."

Kurt Ziegler spread his hands wide. "My brother-in-law, my wife's brother, had such a place. It is just beyond the bathhouse, not far from here, as you know. He died three weeks ago. His wife went home to her folks in Stuttgart. She never liked the place. The hundred marks are paid for this year. You can move in. You and the lady, tonight."

"I do not plan that she will live where I do."

"She lives in your house now."

"She is ill."

"And you must move today."

"So they said."

"They meant it. They had to mean it. As police they could overlook a religious who slept in an unguarded shack. What harm? They could not overlook a man and a woman. My brother was concerned about that. He did not know what you could do. He spoke to me."

"I am grateful. I just don't know—"

"Come along and take a look at it."

"Thank you. I'll tell her first I'm going."

Konrad crossed again to the house, knocked and opened the door. Ursula Vaclav was seated on the floor. She was eating the soup that he had brought.

"I have to leave for a little while," he said. "You'll be all right."

"I want to go to the bathhouse."

"Wait till I come back."

He did not wait for her reply. He joined Kurt Ziegler and they walked down the path to the road and turned right. The Streber Gardens was a community of small houses enclosed by a steel mesh fence. There was a door with a lock. Kurt unlocked it.

"If you move in here," he said, "you can't give keys to

your friends. Your neighbors like it quiet. Some of them do not like talking to people."

"That's all right."

There was a post inside the door, with a bulletin board. It contained messages from management, some personal messages left by people living there and addressed, presumably, to neighbors. The community had a single street. The houses ranged from the simple shack to the small bungalow. Kurt Ziegler stopped at the third house from the gate.

The house was eight feet back from the road, its bulk of land behind it. The entry room, which ran across the house, was a study in tidy untidiness, awkward, ugly garden tools neatly arrayed on shelves and in bins. Behind the room there was a kitchen and, behind that, two bedrooms. The larger bedroom had a double bed and a dresser, the smaller was like a Monk's cell, a straight narrow bed and a chair. There was a small stove in the kitchen that used butane gas and a small, very small, refrigerator.

"I do not deserve such a place," Konrad said.

Kurt laughed. "Take the key," he said. "And hear this. There is a rumor that the lady is your sister, that you are political refugees and that you planned to meet as you did."

"How could there be such a rumor?"

Konrad looked up and there was laughter in Kurt Ziegler's eyes. "A rumor in the hands of a postman will carry far," Kurt said. "If he only tells a few people, they will be the right people."

Konrad shook his head. He did not approve of this rumor but he did not want to argue with it, or discuss it or grant it too much importance. He accepted the key and turned it in his hand.

"I do not know why you should do this for me," he said.

"You are a man in trouble. That is reason enough."

They walked to the gate and parted there. Konrad returned to the house in the clearing. Ursula Vaclav was dressed in baggy trousers such as people in ski resorts might wear and a loose padded coat. She had a hood that was a feminine version of a Monk's hood, white or off-white.

"You took your time," she said. "I have waited forever. Is the bathhouse still open?"

"Yes. For hours yet."

"Good. Walk ahead of me. I'll follow you."

"I want my cart. It has all my gear in it. I'll come back for your bags."

"Why? Where?"

"You'll find out."

He walked into the house. His cart was in the back room, loaded except for a few items. He loaded those items and wheeled the cart into the clearing. Ursula Vaclav was leaning against the wall of the house and he was suddenly concerned about her.

"Are you certain that you can walk?" he said.

"I'll walk. Go ahead of me."

"I'd rather walk with you in case you need help."

"Walk ahead."

Her voice was sharp. He turned his back to her, pushing the cart which, he decided, was a much more pleasant walking companion. He looked back at the end of the path and again where the road met the highway. The girl was walking steadily but there was effort in her walking. He reached the bathhouse and had to wait for her. Her face was pale.

"I may take a long time," she said.

"That is fine. I have errands to do."

"Do them. Do not hurry."

She straightened, seemed to brace herself and entered the bathhouse. He pushed his cart to the Streber Gardens and found a place for his possessions in the room that held garden implements. He took the empty cart back to the clearing and loaded her bags on it. He stowed them in the larger of the two bedrooms, the one with the double bed, and remembered that this was a house which would need groceries.

There was a store, more like a small-town general store than a city establishment. It was a fairly long walk but he walked it, backing a mental wager that it would be open at night. He had only the change from Ursula Vaclav's money and a very little of his own. He debated briefly the ethics of using her money without permission but there seemed to be no alternative. He accepted that lack of an alternative. He was, after all, acting for both of them. He bought carefully, trying to imagine what the girl would like.

It makes no difference about me, he thought. I can eat anything.

He returned to the bathhouse with the groceries in his cart. He did not see Ursula Vaclav so he sat on a fence which commanded a view of the bathhouse door, suddenly aware that he was tired. He waited fifteen minutes. She came out looking subtly different, moving with a vitality which she had lacked previously.

"Sorry if I have kept you waiting," she said.

The sorrow, if she had it, was perfunctory. She did not even look at him. Konrad turned her when she would have headed toward the place in the clearing.

"We have a new home," he said. "If you'll follow me . . ."

"What do you mean, *we* have a *home?*"

She stopped with her hands thrust into the pockets of the

bulky coat she wore, her feet far apart. Her chin was lifted and there was challenge in her.

"The police would not let us stay where we were," Konrad said patiently. "The brother of a policeman offered us another place. You can look at it."

He turned and started walking. She took a couple of quick steps and walked beside him. On the trip over she had insisted that he walk in the lead while she followed. He shook his head, aware of the heavy dusk. He remembered Father Stephen's solemn admonition:

"Never speak to any woman after sunset."

The sun had set and he was speaking to one and there was no cure for it. There was a single lantern-type streetlight beyond the gate of the Streber Gardens and lights in two of the houses on the single street. Konrad opened the gate and the girl hesitated before she followed him to the third house. He walked through the room with the tools and clicked the switch which flowed light over the kitchen, the only living room that the place had. He propped his cart against the wall and turned to face the girl.

"Your room is here," he said.

He opened the door to the larger bedroom and the girl looked in. She could not have missed seeing her bags but she did not comment. "Where is your room?" she said.

"Here."

He opened the door to the small room with its Monk-style bed. The girl stood for a few seconds in the doorway then went to the kitchen. "I have no place else to go. Not tonight," she said. "But I don't know you. Stay out of my room. Don't enter it for any reason, any excuse."

"I am a Monk," he said. "I have my own rules and I obey them."

She stared at him and turned away. "I almost believe that you do," she said. "You bought groceries, didn't you?"

"Yes. I had to use your money, the change from your money."

"Why not? There could not have been much. I'm hungry. I have not cooked for a long time. I will cook if you get out of the kitchen."

"I can help."

"No. Go out. Walk around. Smoke a pipe."

He left the kitchen to her and went outside. It was a calm, quiet night. This place that he had was luxurious to his eyes. He had lived comfortably in Vienna but the place in which he lived had been ugly. There was a softness about this place, a gentle beauty. There were trees down the length of the street, all of them in blossom. The two lighted houses were a bit remote but there was a companionable quality to lights in dwelling places, symbols, somehow, of other people living, breathing, sharing a small patch of earth with one.

He smiled, thinking of the girl's suggestion that he smoke a pipe. He had often thought, watching pipe smokers in Vienna, that there must be relaxation in a pipe, the doing of a meaningless something while one thought of other things. A few, a very few, of the Monks in his group had smoked but Father Stephen had not.

The girl had been speaking German tonight. He had not been aware of it at the time, responding automatically to the language spoken, but he was aware of it now, remembering their conversational exchange. There was a slight accent on her German although she spoke it better than she spoke Russian. She had probably decided to abandon the pretense that she was Russian when she was faced with the necessity of writing a note. She had written in German. This all seemed melodramatic, the kind of thing that young people talked about in Vienna; spies and espionage and secret intelligence, lives lived in code. He had heard much of such talk but if he had ever met a spy he had been unaware of it.

It was strange that he was more sharply aware of Ursula Vaclav's language when he was away from her than he had been when he was listening to her. It struck him with a sense of mild shock that he did not have any mental picture of her. He remembered a blue blouse with white polka dots in it that she wore when he first saw her. She had buried her face in her hands and there had been a ripped place in the right sleeve. He remembered the ski-type slacks she wore tonight and the padded jacket and the white hood. He remembered impressions that he had, that she seemed tired or pale, but he could not see in his mind the face that had been pale, nor any feature of that face.

He had had an overall first impression that this woman was unattractive, ugly, unlikable. The impression hung suspended in his mind, not anchored to anything and he concentrated, trying to see her. When he brought her to his place in the clearing and set her down in the big room, her facial skin had been red, blotchy, her hair in untidy disorder, her face puffy. Beyond that he could not bring back any detail of face or form. She was not a heavy woman. He had picked her up and carried her when they came to the place in the clearing.

He walked into the house and she was standing beside the stove. He was in the darkness of the room with the tools, looking into the light. She had changed her clothes. She was wearing a striped blouse, blue stripes on white, and a dark skirt. The blouse was open at the throat and it had short sleeves. She was a slender girl, younger than he would have thought if he had given thought to her probable age. She was wearing a light scarf over her hair, tied under her chin. Her eyes seemed dark. She had a wide mouth with a prominent lower lip. Her eyebrows looked pencil-shaped and they were unnaturally black, but she did not seem to be wearing any other make-up, not even lipstick.

His foot scraped and she heard him. Her head came up and her eyes were frightened momentarily. She snapped her fingers then, an odd gesture. "You can come in," she said. "Dinner is ready."

She had scrambled eggs and minced in with them some of the *Bierwurst* he had bought. He would have bought ham if he had had enough money, but the *Bierwurst* had a rich aroma of its own. She had sliced the bread and laid butter on the table. Butter was one of the luxuries that he had added to his order on her account, with the thought that she might like it. He had bought milk, too, and cocoa. Coffee and tea were out of his habit and beyond his purse.

"It is a very fine supper," the girl said stiffly. "Thank you."

"Thank you for cooking it."

Konrad felt awkward, uncomfortable. Other women had served him meals in kitchens and there had been no self-consciousness, no embarrassment. The women had been in their own kitchens and he had had a temporary place in their homes as an itinerant Monk. This situation was different. He did not have a clearly defined role and neither did the girl. They ate their supper quietly without conversation. Konrad pushed his chair back.

"I will wash the dishes," he said.

"You don't have to do so."

"It is a fair division. You cooked and I will wash dishes."

"I will not argue with that. I am tired." The girl rose, swayed a little and checked the swaying with the tips of her fingers against the tabletop. "I will be leaving in the morning. I cannot do it tonight."

"You need not leave until you are well, until you feel strong." He hesitated. "I will not give you any reason to hate me."

The girl pushed against the table, turned and walked toward the larger bedroom. "There is not a woman in the world who would not hate a man who had seen her as you saw me," she said.

It was her good night to him and he thought about it as he washed and dried the dishes. He thought about it when he walked out into the garden. The lamp at the gate still threw a soft line of light along the street but there was no longer light behind the windows of houses. The night was cloudy now with few stars.

It would be easier, he thought, and more comfortable if the girl left in the morning, but he distrusted easy, comfortable answers to anything. She had been very ill. She had forced herself to meet the day and she had walked to the bathhouse, but those were feats of will. She was still not fit and, on such evidence as he had, she had no place to go. He did not know how the community of Streber Gardens would act toward her, or toward himself. Their presence might be resented merely because they were strangers, or the elements of scandal might color the situation if there were people who sought scandal.

He sat on the ground and raised his eyes to the stars beyond the thin veil of cloud. He addressed his prayer to God, as he always did, stating his problem as he saw it and asking for a solution to it. He waited then, forming no thoughts or images of his own, motionless for an hour. No answer came to him; nothing at all.

Chapter Three

The U. S. Army shack in the clearing had a bleak, deserted appearance in the early morning. Konrad looked at it and felt no identity with it. Yesterday it had been his home. He had no explanation for his change of feeling and he normally spent little time on things for which he lacked an explanation. He had brought a spade in his cart and there was a mop in the shack. He mopped the floor first and it needed mopping. Ursula Vaclav had tried to take care of it but her strength had not measured up to the task that she had set for herself. He found her effort rather pathetic.

There was a wadded package at the clearing edge, under the trees. He had expected to find it. These were the clothes she had worn. She had had nothing that she could do with them, of course, so she had hidden them. They were beyond any further use. Konrad dug a hole and buried them. He was patting the last layer of soil into place above the package when he heard a footstep.

Otto entered the clearing through the trees on the lower end. He was a graceless youth who shambled rather than walked, a youth whose hair was untidy and whose expression was sullen. Watching him cross the clearing,

Konrad felt again that sense of antagonism which the youth had originally awakened in him, such an antagonism as he rarely felt for a human being. In this case it was unjust, certainly. Without Otto's aid he would not have been able to handle a problem which he had voluntarily undertaken.

"I wondered if you would be here," Otto said. "I am on my way to school."

"Nice of you to stop."

"I thought you might need me for something, might need help or need some job done or—"

Otto's voice trailed off. Konrad looked at him, sympathizing with the inarticulate quality. This lad had changed in many ways, but perhaps not greatly. The crude language, the repetition of a meaningless phrase, those, too, had been inarticulate things. Below the surface it was difficult to imagine what Otto might be like.

"I'd like to help you," Otto said. "I was wrong about you at first. You're different than anybody I know." It was obviously difficult for him to continue but he looked away from Konrad toward the trees, seeming to brace himself. "Maybe I can learn something from you. In all my life I've never learned anything."

"That's an exaggeration. Of course you have."

"I haven't. And I don't know what I want to learn. I don't know."

There was a certain desperation in the boy's voice, in his expression, in the forward thrust of his body. Konrad sensed the desperation, feeling helpless in the face of it.

"I'm not a teacher," he said. "I would be glad to ask you for help when I'm working on something, but you wouldn't learn much. The learning would have to start way back where I cannot take you."

"Everything does. That's why I can't learn. Nothing starts now, where I am."

Otto's desperation was contagious; Konrad could feel it taking hold of him. It was his desperation, too. He lacked a connecting link with these young boys who had grown up in a world of different values, of different ideals, of different experience. Otto became suddenly aware of time.

"I'm late," he said. "I wrote my address on a paper. Here it is. I'd like to see you again."

"I'm in Streber Gardens, third house from the gate. If there's a light in the house call my name. I'll be home evenings."

"That woman, is she there?"

"Yes. Until she is well again."

"Oh."

Otto turned abruptly and was gone. Konrad picked up his gear. He thought now, while making a last survey of the U. S. Army shack, that he could see why he failed with last night's prayer. He had prayed sincerely and he had sought for a way in which he could help Ursula Vaclav. If prayer was merely a seeking for an easy solution to difficulty, a means of transferring one's own responsibility to someone else, then prayer would inevitably lack an answer.

Father Stephen had told him while he was still a small boy that, quite often, prayers went unanswered, that one should never rebel against the silence but should seek humbly for the reason behind it, contributing to the growth of his own soul in the seeking.

"Never seek that reason on the night when you pray into the silence," Father Stephen said. "The hours that belong to sleep must be given to sleep. All things in their place. Set an hour on the following morning and when that hour comes, return to the problem."

As with so much of Father Stephen's teaching, this seemed the essence of simplicity until one sought to practice it. It had taken Konrad years to learn how to examine prayer, as it had taken him years to learn how to pray; and he still felt like an uneasy pilgrim—standing at the gate of mysteries.

Last night he had set as his time for seeking an answer the hour in which his work in this clearing would be finished. The answer had been building within him for half an hour and now it commanded his attention. He was strapping the spade to his cart and he stopped.

He could feel the presence of Otto still in the clearing and he could hear Father Stephen's voice.

"Do not ask God to do for you what you can do for yourself."

He stood motionless, his fingers still on the strap that bound the spade. Certainly! He had sought an answer to the problem of the boys one night, an answer to the problem of Ursula Vaclav another night, not facing either problem himself. Life had been simple in the monastery: events had moved smoothly, for the most part, in preordained grooves. There had been basic principles, fundamental truths, in which one could put faith.

"Every day in your life is a day in school," Father Stephen said. "One takes many things from a school but one attends it, primarily, in order to learn."

As he often did, Father Stephen had forgotten his audience. Konrad had not understood that message when he heard it because Konrad had no knowledge of schools, no experience with them. The monastery, of course, had been his school but no one ever referred to it as a school and Konrad did not make the connection until he was grown, until he was working in Vienna.

The boys, each of them, had presented him with problems to solve. So had Ursula Vaclav. They were his problems. They were his opportunity to learn. Why had he scoffed mentally at Otto who claimed, quite honestly, that he could not learn? He, Konrad, had the same difficulty. It was all very simple. He would have a serious talk with Werner and one with Otto. Tonight he would talk to Ursula Vaclav and make her see that the solving of her problem was her own task, that he would help where he could but that there was a limit to what he could do. There would be no problems once he had faced them, none at all. The answer lay in facing them.

He was happy at the manner in which isolated patterns of thought had fallen into place. He rolled the featherbed and secured it with the two strands of rope that had come with it. It had escaped damage, thanks to the plastic covering but it was a heavy, awkward, difficult burden. He put it on his cart and had a problem in securing it there. The cart was almost impossible to lift and propel with the extra weight added and he had to strain to see around the bulk in front of him.

The journey to the home of the man for whom he had restored the painting was longer than he remembered. It was a relief when he reached it and rolled his burden down. The old man was friendly, vaguely friendly, making little of the loan of mattress and mop. All that Konrad had in common with the man was the one painting and the topic was exhausted. He had made the same discovery before in connection with people. He often touched a life lightly on one surface spot, moving on without leaving any trace of his passing upon the life itself.

He whistled as he pushed the cart down the road, feeling it light and easy now to his touch. He would, he decided, abandon the suburbs, at least for the day, and try his fortune in the city proper. There was money in the city and he would be in trouble, grave trouble, if he did not earn some money.

He found his job at 11:15.

He was walking on a long street in the city. There was a slender building ahead of him and on his left, a building with a cross on it. The building had tall rectangular windows that suggested classrooms. On the third floor there was a nun in a gray habit and full bonnet standing on the window ledge, outside, washing a window. She had no protective strap and the space behind her was a sheer drop. She wielded a sponge vigorously, bending to dip into an invisible bucket at intervals.

Konrad stood watching her. This was something that he could not do, but something that he could understand: this was Faith.

He had been avoiding Roman Catholic institutions in Germany but this seemed a likely place to step over the line again. A young nun with quiet eyes opened the door for him, ushered him into an overfurnished, overdecorated parlor and told him that she would speak to the Mother Superior. Konrad seated himself, pleased that he had worn his black robe today. It made him a part of the atmosphere in which he found himself.

The Mother Superior was a tall woman. She could have been any age. Her face had a sculpted beauty, without any revealing expression. Her eyes were gray. She heard his explanation that he was a Russian Monk and the brief, condensed catalog of his skills.

"I did not anticipate that you would be a Russian," she said, "but I knew that you would arrive. When we have a need it is answered. Come!"

She led the way into the chapel and indicated the Stations of the Cross with the gesture of a slim hand. One of the Stations was missing and, at a casual glance, several of the others were damaged. Konrad looked closely at the Seventh Station, Jesus Falls the Second Time. There were four figures in the scene, the fallen Saviour and three belligerent Romans. The original carver had been a good craftsman, not an artist. His figures were standard figures conscientiously done. He had worked in lime, an excellent wood for sculpture and, on the walls of such a chapel as this, his scenes were impressive. It was a large chapel, obviously serving a school.

"There is a workroom," the Mother Superior said.

The workroom was, inevitably, in the basement and without a window. There was a carpenter's bench underneath a two-bulb ceiling lamp. The missing Station of the Cross was on the tabletop, clamped in place. It was Station Six, Veronica Wipes the Face of Jesus.

"We had a man who planned to repair all of our Stations," the Mother Superior said, "but he had a problem. As you can see, he left in mid-work."

"I see."

The unknown workman had gone lightly on the use of wax. He had carved small pieces to replace those that had been broken; notably the fingers and the arm of Veronica. His hand had been shaky. There were small nicks and rough places.

"You are not impressed? You can do better?" the nun asked.

"Yes."

"I believe you. I like a dash of arrogance with humility. As I estimate it you should have two months of work on our Stations. If you are faster, we have other work that you can do. I will expect you at eight in the morning and you must be out of the building before five. Now, how much will that cost us a day?"

Konrad had always had difficulty with the fixing of a

price on his work. He had no goal for his earnings. He asked only to live. Restoring beauty out of ugliness or damage or decay was a reward in itself. He fixed a price and the Mother Superior's eyes met his coldly.

"My dear young Russian," she said. "You have quoted a price for your work that is exactly one half what this other man charged us. That man, I might add, was underpaid. I am going to pay you double what you asked. You will be paid at the close of every day and on this first day I shall pay you for three days. You will always be two days in our debt. Is that satisfactory?"

"More than satisfactory."

"No! Not more. Do not forget your arrogance. It is essential to an artist. Your luncheon will be served here in twenty minutes."

The Mother Superior nodded curtly and glided away, moving without sound. He was aware of her still after she had gone. That nun on the window sill was comprehensible now, standing unprotected on a narrow ledge that was probably wet with soapy water.

"She was probably ordered to do it," he said.

His luncheon arrived in exactly twenty minutes and it was a good luncheon. He was left alone then through a long afternoon. He finished all of Station Six except the face of Veronica which had been flattened by some blunt object. The other man had, of course, taken his tools, leaving only the clamps and several varieties of good glue. The clamps had probably belonged with the table in the first place.

At 4:40 the Mother Superior returned. She looked at the work on the tabletop. Her face conveyed no expression of approval or disapproval.

"I see that you found that arm of Veronica beyond your tolerance," she said, "as I did."

"I replaced it."

"And quite well. You will work out happily here and we shall be fortunate in having you. Do you drink?"

"I am a Monk."

"A half answer. There have been cases. Never mind. Your predecessor's problems came in bottles."

She took a white envelope from some recess in her habit and extended it. "One of the nuns will bring you an envelope each day at this time," she said. "I shall probably not see you again."

He accepted the envelope. "Thank you. I'm grateful."

"No gratitude, please. There is a fair exchange between us or there is no honesty. Good night."

Konrad's eyes followed her as she left the room. His fingers tightened on the envelope and he could feel the money inside it. He had three days' pay at more than he had ever expected to earn per day. He walked back to the streets and the crowds were in them. The sky was crimson and he could see two churches with oniontop steeples as he walked west. He remembered what Father Stephen had said about oniontop steeples in the sunset.

"They are the Biblical tongues of flame," he said.

Chapter Four

There was a cooking fragrance in the house at Streber Gardens. It floated out to the gate and Konrad stood for a moment, sniffing it. The walk from the convent had been four miles and he had been pushing a cart. The toil of the day, too, was in his muscles.

The table was set in the kitchen and it had a small bottle of the German white wine, the Liebfraumilch, standing in the middle of it. There was veal cooking and vegetables. Ursula Vaclav stood beside the stove, solemn and unsmiling. Konrad's gesture took in all of the kitchen.

"Where?" he said.

"A store. I found it. It was a long walk."

"I had a long walk, too. I did not expect anything like this."

"I did it for myself more than for you. I wanted something nice."

He had no answer to that. He went into the small lavatory and washed. When he came out there were meat and vegetables on his plate and the girl was sitting on the facing side of the table. He stood in his place, made the Sign of the Cross and prayed over the food that was his. The girl watched him, making no move to join his prayer. When he seated himself, she smiled faintly.

"I hope that you made some money today," she said. "I spent nearly all of mine for this."

"I made a lot of money."

He told her about the nun washing windows, about the Stations needing repair, of his conversation with the nun. He did not tell her that his own price for his services had been too low. It was pleasant to have someone who would listen to the day when it had been such an interesting day. He opened the wine and poured it. Wine had been taken for granted with meals in the monastery except in periods of fasting and in hard times. Fasting periods had been many and so had the hard times. He and Stephen had been poor and when they could afford wine he let Stephen have it. Wine therefore was part of his life yet not part of it. He liked it tonight.

The girl was not wearing her scarf. Her hair was dark, very dark, probably black. Her eyes were an odd shade. They might, he thought, be called hazel which was yellowish brown, but that was not accurate either. They were luminous eyes. There was a softness about her that he had not noticed before. He could not define the softness; he merely felt that it was there.

Konrad drank the last of his wine. "I have never had a finer meal in my life," he said.

"You exaggerate, of course, but I am happy if you liked it." Ursula Vaclav leaned forward, her forearms resting against the table edge. "You see, I did not fix this dinner just for me. It was a penance, sort of a penance. I had to do something because I hated you so deeply."

She let the words fall, without emphasis. He stared at her, then made a half-gesture of protest. "You have no reason."

"Oh, but I have." Her small hands tightened into fists on the tabletop. "You went back to that other house today, didn't you?"

"Of course. I had to put it in shape."

"You did it while I slept. You knew that I was ashamed. I told you that any woman would hate a man who had seen her as you saw me. You made it worse. You went back. I wanted to clean that place."

"You were not strong enough to do it. You have been very ill."

"That's why I walked to that store, to prove you wrong, to prove that I am strong enough." She straightened her body and there was a strange stillness in her. "There was a package," she said, "a small, or not so small, embarrassing package, a bundle. I hid it under a tree. I had no place else. You found it. No one else would have touched it."

"I buried it," he said. "It was the thing to do."

She pushed her chair back from the table. "I'll hate you as long as I live," she said.

She ran away then, ran into her own room. Konrad rose slowly. There was nothing that he could do about her. He remembered his resolve of the morning. It had seemed so simple then. He was going to have a quiet talk with her and settle everything. He could not even remember now what problems he had planned to solve.

He cleared the table and was rinsing the dishes in the sink when the girl came back. "I will wash the dishes," she said. "It is my job."

"No. It is fair that one person cooks and the other one cleans up."

"No."

She pushed him aside and took over the dishwashing. He picked up a dishrag and dried the dishes as they emerged from the hot water. She ignored his activity as she ignored him until the dishes were clean and stacked away.

"I should not have spoken as I did," she said. "I should not have brought the subject up. I ruined the dinner."

There was a slight catch in her voice. "You did not ruin the dinner," he said. "It was a wonderful dinner. I understand how you feel."

"You couldn't understand how I feel. Never mind. It is done. I am under obligation to you. I should be grateful. I have to ask more favors. You are entitled to explanations."

"I do not want explanations."

"You shall have them. You knew that I was not Russian?"

"Of course. There are over three hundred languages or dialects or tongues in Russia. I have not heard all of them but you were not speaking any of them. I am certain of that."

"I am a Czech. My father is a Czech but his parents were Russian. He considers himself Russian but he has never been there."

"You learned from him?"

"Yes. My mother's name is Vania. She is part Hungarian, part Slav. They are very simple people. They live in Kladno. It is the place in which I was born. My father is a very minor executive in the Iron Works. He has little money but he has dignity. The dignity means much to him."

The girl was forgetting herself while she talked. The lines of tension vanished from her face. She used her hands dramatically when she wanted to emphasize a point but she seemed unconscious that she was doing so. Her eyes warmed remembering her parents. Her mouth was wide but it was expressive. She had beauty of a sort. Konrad had not suspected that.

"Enough," she said. "I am a peasant inside of me. I feel it. I do not want to be but I am. A Czechoslovakian peasant can be horrible, not at all as writers write of him. I am well educated. It hides the peasant part. I went to college in Prague. I taught school. I developed a sympathy. It made a specialist of me." Her eyes seemed far away; suddenly they came back. Her body straightened. "Am I boring you?"

"Far from it."

"Thank you. I want to talk. Something. It wasn't the wine. We didn't have much wine. A small bottle for two people. Where was I? Oh, yes. My specialty. I became interested in poor children who are retarded, who do not learn as others do, who cannot do naturally the things other children do. People just hid them away. It was cruel. There were so few teachers who would work with them. I volunteered. I worked in a special school."

She broke off abruptly, rose and walked around the room. "When I talk like this, when I have someone to listen, I wish that I smoked cigarettes. I never have smoked them, but I have watched people. Smoking makes it easier to talk, I am certain."

She came back to her chair, ran her hand through her hair, then stared at her hand as she opened and closed it. "There was a high official, very high, big in politics in Czechoslovakia. He had two small children, a boy and a girl, children of much charm, wonderful in appearance but retarded. There are many such. They are victims of the war even though they were not born until many years after it was over. He employed me, this politician. I would teach his children. I would be the governess. I liked the children. He said that I would travel. I had never been outside Czechoslovakia."

She spread her hands wide. "We came to Munich, this

man and his wife and the children and me. I did not know it, but it was his way of escape from Czechoslovakia where, maybe, he was not too safe any more with the Russians. I do not know. He defected. He left in a night, with my hotel room paid for only one day. He left me a little money in an envelope, not much money, a very little. There was no note, no good-bye, no anything. I do not know where they went."

She snapped her fingers. "I talk too much."

"No. You are interesting. What did you do?"

"I had a cold. I felt ill, but it was an expensive hotel. I could not afford to stay in it. I had this name of a woman, and an address, a friend of my mother, or anyway someone she knew. Somebody told me how to go. I took a streetcar and I became very ill."

She lifted her shoulders, spreading her hands apart. "The rest you know."

"Yes. Your politician was a scoundrel."

"There are many scoundrels. So now I am sitting in your house. I have no right to be here."

"It is not my house."

"That only makes it more difficult. I am in Germany. I have no right to be in Germany either."

"Why not?"

"I have a limited passport, for a governess, employed and traveling, not permitted to live or work in the country visited. I am no longer employed by this politician. Would Germany let me stay and work?"

Konrad shook his head. She was in a worse position than a Stateless person. She was someone who definitely belonged in another country, someone vaguely suspicious because of a connection with a foreign politician out of favor in his own government. Germany would ship her back.

The girl was watching his face. She seemed to read his thought. "I must go back to Czechoslovakia," she said. "I have nowhere else. I want to go quietly, with no talk of politics or politicians. If I may stay here a few days I will write to my mother and ask her to send me a letter. If she will write to me and say that she needs me at home, I will show the letter at the border and have no trouble."

Konrad nodded. "Yes," he said. "That is the simplest way. Simple solutions are the ones that work. You may stay here as long as you like if they let me stay here."

"Thank you."

The girl rose and the talk was over. He remembered what she had said about her father's dignity. She, too, had dignity under difficult circumstances.

"I always pray for over an hour before I go to bed," he said, "and I prefer to pray out of doors. Do not be alarmed if you hear me moving around."

"I won't be."

It was an exceptionally dark night and the air had moisture in it. Konrad walked back and forth as a preface to prayer. He had had a fortunate day. He had two months of work ahead of him, fascinating work, at a wage that seemed impressive. He was comfortably housed and he had had a memorable dinner.

He thought about the girl. The man who had employed her to care for his children was a scoundrel. He had abandoned her in a strange city as some people abandoned small animals, not caring what happened to her. She was a strange girl. She was not religious. She had not joined him in his prayer of thanks for the food that they ate, yet she had dedicated herself to the teaching of retarded children because they needed what few people gave.

His prayer of the night was a prayer of gratitude for all that he had received, for all that he possessed. He did not offer problems for solutions or ask questions. He had, he believed, been blessed beyond his deserving and had no right to ask for more.

He had a sense of a presence sharing the lonely darkness with him while he prayed but the screen of his mind remained blank. Nothing came back to him from his prayer save the assurance that he was not alone; that, of course, was enough.

Chapter Five

The clouds fell apart in the night and the rain spilled out. It fell straight down with no wind touching it and continued to fall for hours. It was beating with a steady rhythm against the house when Konrad awakened. He had had one room at the monastery for about a year in which it was a joy to listen to rain, a room with multiple echoes. He wanted to lie and listen to this rain but he took three deep breaths and rolled out. Once on his feet, the day was started.

He wrote a brief note to Ursula Vaclav and enclosed a third of yesterday's money in an envelope for her. He donned his heavy black robe, the only garment he had that was suitable for the day, and pulled the peaked hood over his head. He had four miles to walk and he would appear, he knew, like a figure out of the Middle Ages walking those miles. The idea amused him.

Halfway to the convent he stopped in a small restaurant and ate his breakfast. It was an extravagance and restaurants were out of his normal pattern but he was wet and cold and the breakfast was richly satisfying. He barely noticed the rain on the last half of his journey. There was, as he had anticipated, a service entrance to the convent. A glum-looking janitor admitted him and he saw no one else. Someone had saved him a trip to the chapel. The next Station on which he was to work was standing beside his table. It was a dull Station, Number Seven, Jesus Falls the Second Time. There was no challenge in it; merely three brutal Roman soldiers and a figure on the ground.

He worked patiently through the day, eating his lunch when it came and surprised when the nun brought his wages in an envelope. He had not talked to anyone all day so he smiled at her.

"The day passed swiftly," he said.

"*Ja.* And tomorrow is Saturday. You do not come."

"Nor Sunday?"

"Never."

It was not exactly a conversation but it was, at least, a human exchange. Konrad donned his black robes and went back to the city streets. It was no longer raining and one had to look diligently for evidence that rain had fallen. There were more people on the streets than there had been on yesterday.

Konrad was surprised that it was Friday. He did not own a calendar and had never owned one. In the monastery one always knew what day it was and which saint, or saints, were to be honored. Father Stephen had carried a rough time chart in his brain and he knew the principal feasts without consulting almanacs or calendars. Konrad, who had never known the need for personally keeping track of time, had no days in his week. Sunday was the Sabbath but that did not worry him because he tried to keep every day holy. In Vienna, when he was employed, he kept track necessarily of working days and now, it seemed, he would have to do that again.

There was an air of excitement, a sense of color and

movement in the street that led home. The gate to Streber Gardens was open and men and women moved in and out. There were many bicycles. This, Konrad thought, was testimony to the fact that the day was Friday. The people of the Gardens were, for the most part, weekenders. They had to be poor people to qualify for a small spot of ground there and that accounted for the bicycles. There would be no automobiles and most of the people would probably consider streetcars expensive. Konrad looked at the people with interest: young for the most part but with a fair balance out of the middle or late years. They seemed friendly, companionable with one another, happy with their weekend holiday.

Werner was waiting for him outside the gate. He was dressed in his usual fashion but, in some intangible way, he looked neater. His hair was combed. He had thick dark hair. He looked relaxed, not angry at anyone, and the effect was pleasant. He was a handsome young man.

"Hello," Konrad said. "I thought I had lost you."

"The shoe belongs on the other foot. I lost you."

"I had no time to send out notifications. Will you come in to my place?"

"I have been in it. It is very nice. I met her. She doesn't like me."

"She doesn't know you."

"Never mind. It makes no difference. I wanted to tell you that I have been lucky. At least, I think so. Maybe not."

"Tell me."

"It is very simple. You talked about museums. I didn't know much about them. You said that I should practice drawing. I could not copy fine paintings. I went to the Deutsches Museum. It is fascinating, a place of machines and instruments. I was sketching some old bottles, crazy shapes, in the apothecary shop when a man asked me if I would do some sketches for him."

"What kind of man?"

"I don't know. Old. Fairly old. A foreigner. He speaks German like a foreigner. It isn't important. He has a notebook. He makes notes. He cannot sketch. He will pay me to make sketches, copies of things. I don't have to be as good as I would like to be. He is interested in old farm tools. I did a sketch of a plow for him, a ridiculous-looking plow."

"How much work does he have for you?"

Werner shrugged. "I don't know. I could make more money on Rubble Hill. I like doing this. My parents don't like it."

"Why not?"

"They do not understand it. If they do not understand something they dislike it."

"Maybe they are afraid that you will be wasting your time."

"I won't be wasting my time."

Konrad had been studying Werner as they talked. The boy had always had assurance of a sort but it had not been tied to anything. The discovery of one talent of his own, one skill, had given him a sense of direction. He was not thinking of anyone else. He had reached a decision as to what he wanted to do and he did not think beyond that.

Konrad found this development interesting, far more interesting than anything Werner might say. The boy had had the quality of leadership when he first saw him and the ability to arrive at decisions was inherent in leadership, but it was still interesting to see it develop.

"I'll have to be going now," Werner said. "I just wanted you to know."

"Thanks. I'll walk along a short distance. I want to ask you something."

"Fine. Ask! I probably won't know."

"You'll know. Now that you've found yourself, I won't have to worry about you. How about Otto? What can I do for him?"

"Nothing. I've been trying to help him. I'm the only one. It's just too damned difficult."

"Why?"

"He's got a problem. He doesn't want to be what he thinks he is."

Konrad digested that. It was a cryptic remark. He was fairly certain that he understood it. It would not do, at any rate, to ask for an explanation.

"What do you think about him?"

Werner shrugged. "He is probably right. I'm not that way, not a little bit. He knows it. He is all right when he's with me. I can't nurse him but I've tried to keep him away from people who could be trouble to him. I wasn't sure about you at first."

"Me?"

"Right. The Monk stuff did not seem real. Anyway, you're all right. Nobody can straighten out Otto."

"Why not?"

"Lots of reasons. For one thing, his mother isn't married. That makes a difference around here. Strict people. Religious. He hates not having a father. His mother is a terrible woman. Otto can't get away from her."

"She can't be so terrible. She sent over soup for my patient when I needed it badly."

Werner laughed. "She never sent any soup to anybody. Otto does most of the cooking in that house. He sent it."

Konrad stared at him. This was something that he would never have suspected, a sharper picture of Otto, perhaps, than Werner realized. Werner was absorbed in himself now and Werner might hold to the direction he had found, but Otto very definitely was going to need help, one way or another.

"I've walked far enough," Konrad said. "I'll go back now."

He stood straight when he stopped walking and Werner, who had taken two steps beyond him, had to turn back. For the first time today he was off balance, out of command of the situation.

"I hope you do well with your sketches," Konrad said. "I will pray for you."

Werner's eyes widened slightly. "Yes," he said. "All right. Pray for me. Thanks."

He wheeled and hurried away. Konrad turned back. He had much to think about but he was suddenly tired. There were people in the street which bisected the Gardens but they managed to ignore the fact that he was passing by. He could understand that. He was not a neighbor. He had not established himself.

The dinner was fragrant again and there was a small bottle of white wine. Ursula Vaclav raised her eyebrows when she saw him.

"Who was he, that boy?" she said.

"Somebody named Werner. He may be an artist some day."

"He will not wait for some day. He will be happy with himself now."

"He is young. It might be a sad thing if he was too sensible too soon."

Konrad went in to wash the dust of the road away. His dinner was served and in his place when he came to the table. He said grace over it and the girl watched him silently. She did not speak until he was opening the wine.

"You did mean for me to shop for dinner when you left that money this morning?" she said. "Or didn't you?"

"It was for you. I meant for you to do anything that you wanted to do with it. We had already spent your money."

"Mostly on me. It was a very little. I have no right to your money."

He smiled. "You live in this place. It is a monastery. We provide hospitality. We have more money today."

He laid his salary on the table. The girl looked at it. "I have money left from this morning," she said.

It was stiff, awkward conversation. They were further apart than the width of the table but there was no way of narrowing the distance. He was aware of the girl now as a person but he did not know how to talk to her. She no longer looked gaunt and sharp-featured. There was a soft smoothness to her skin and she had done something to her hair; it was full and uncurled but it formed a gentle frame for her face.

Immediately after they had finished the dishes, she turned toward her own room. "I will say good night," she said.

The door of her room clicked shut and he was aware of disappointment. He would have liked to talk to her, to listen while she talked. He walked to the door. It was early and there were lights in most of the houses, a movement of people. They would not settle down early. It would be difficult to pray without silence but not impossible. A masculine voice called out and another masculine voice answered. Konrad did not hear what they said but the tone was friendly. He had known such friendly masculine exchanges for years in the monastery, had known them with Father Stephen and on the streets in Vienna. He missed all of that as he missed reading. He had not done any reading in months.

He sat down, surrendering himself to the night, preparing for prayer, not praying. He had not been able to talk to Ursula Vaclav tonight. He had had, of course, little experience in talking with women. Even in Vienna his experience of women had been meager.

The old flat in which he lived with Father Stephen was on a poor street, one of the narrow, shadowy streets on the very edge of brightness and gaiety. There were prostitutes who lived on that street and some of the streets adjoining. There was no mistaking what they were once a man learned that there were prostitutes in the world. There was certainly no reticence on their part when it came to proclaiming their trade. They thought it amusing that Konrad, a Monk who walked wide of them, was living where they lived. Some of them mocked him or made jokes when they passed him and some of them greeted him with obscenities, but they were not unfriendly. They learned eventually to take him for granted as he took them for granted.

There was one night when he came home late. The building which housed him was four stories high. He and Stephen lived on the third floor. There was a rectangular space on the ground floor where once itinerant musicians played and the space projected upward to the skylight with a banistered walkaround on each floor. On this one night there was a girl sitting on the stairs at the second landing.

She was a young girl, blonde, in a yellow dress. Konrad knew her by sight as one of the prostitutes but he had never spoken to her. She was seated in the middle of the step so that he could not pass her. She raised her head, looking up at him. The light in the hall was dim but he had the impression that she had been crying. She moved over slightly, patting the seat beside her.

"Won't you sit here with me a little while?" she said.

He was startled and he had no words. He could only stare at her. The girl patted the step again, impatiently. "I won't hurt you," she said. "I know you don't want me. That's why I'd like to talk to you. I'd like to talk to a man who isn't a pimp or a customer."

He seated himself beside her awkwardly. "I don't know what to say."

"Anything, anything at all. I'll listen."

Thought seemed to come to a complete stop and he had no words. He was aware of the scent that the girl wore, a strong scent, and ever after that he would be aware of that scent when girls entered his dreams. He was aware, too, of another subtler scent that was not a scent at all, a scent that he associated with a woman because it had not existed in the monastery.

"I've never seen anyone sitting on these steps before," he said.

"People do. Lovers."

She waited and he swallowed hard, seeking desperately for words, any kind of words. The question in his mind was, Why are you a prostitute? but he rejected it as too personal.

"How old are you?" he said.

"Nearly twenty. I'll be twenty next month."

It was a solemn thought that she was only twenty. She seemed to be waiting again and he was aware that she was watching him although he did not look at her.

"I am from Russia," he said.

The statement took her by surprise. "It is a long way, Russia," she said. "I am of Vienna, only Vienna."

She was not interested in him or she would ask questions

herself. She had probably lost all interest in men as persons and missed their interest in herself. The men she met were interested in her body and did not even see her, probably, as a human being. She wanted to be something else besides a body. Konrad sensed that, dimly, not certain that he was correct. In spite of himself, without his consciously willing it, the question uppermost in his mind came out.

"Why are you a prostitute?" he said.

She drew away from him slightly. "Everyone asks that," she said. "It's nobody's business. Nobody has a right to know. Hell! It's simple, I guess. What we do is something they've got to do and they need someone to do it with."

"I'm sorry I asked. I didn't do you any good. I am not a good conversationalist."

"No. You're not. Never mind. You tried."

She waved her hand. It was clearly a dismissal signal. He rose awkwardly, standing for a moment above her. She did not look up. He climbed the stairs and from the banister railing on the third floor he looked down at her, a study of bowed head and hunched shoulders on the shadowed step.

He saw her many nights after that on the street but she never gave any sign of recognition. There was no meaning in the meetings but the memory of a thin, inadequate exchange of words remained with him. He could see her still, sitting alone where he left her. He had not even asked her her name.

Chapter Six

The men of the Gardens worked out of doors on Sunday afternoon. They worked in the soil or they did simple carpenter work or they touched up porches or shutters with paint. Many of them had women working with them and there was no sense of pressure or hurry in anything they did. Konrad, from his own yard, could see them up and down the street and he envied them. He had never had what they had although his life had been rich in other ways. No work had been done in the monastery on Sunday but he had participated in endless rounds of ritual and, sometimes, he read books. In Vienna he had had housework to do on Sunday, work that he had to neglect through the week. Here, he felt restless. Ursula Vaclav had cooked chicken and vegetables. She was doing the dishes now, refusing his offer to dry them.

He looked helplessly at the growing stuff in the small garden. He did not know what it was nor what to do with it. He saw other men wielding hoes and he moved his own hoe around aimlessly, not understanding the purpose of the tool. The girl came out and watched him for minutes before he discovered her.

"The monastery had no garden? No farm?" she said.

"Yes. It did in fact. It produced its own food but the work was the work of brothers. Monks who came from farms, dedicated men but not priests."

"You were not one of them."

"No. I had other work."

"You were a priest?"

"No. I did much common labor. I studied."

"Well, give me the hoe. I know more about it than you do."

He turned the tool over and watched her while she wielded it. She obviously knew what she was doing and she had been prepared to do it. She was wearing blue overall-type slacks and a gray shirt. It embarrassed him that she was more capable than he. Looking back on his life in the monastery, he could see that there had been a shaping, that he had been trained in the arts, in the very finest work that Monks did. Father Stephen had, of course, been responsible for that and he was not a man who worked or planned aimlessly. Father Stephen had had a purpose in mind, an aim for Konrad, but he had never revealed it and circumstances, obviously, had derailed his plan, whatever it was.

Konrad walked through the house to the small yard in front. There was a stocky man standing at the gate, a light-haired man with a bushy mustache which drooped downward at either side of his mouth. The man wore a wide-brimmed black hat and a dark jacket.

"Are you the Monk, Konrad?" he said.

"I am."

"I'm Ludwig Rohne."

When the man saw that Konrad did not find any significance in his name, he added: "I'm Werner's father."

"Oh. I'm sorry."

"Didn't know his name, did you? Well, that's like him.

Not very proud of his name or his family or anything he's got. I've been wanting to meet you."

"I'm happy to meet you. Won't you come in?"

"No. I think not. You have a woman here, haven't you?"

"She's been ill. She will probably leave tomorrow."

"I'd rather talk to you and leave the women out of it. I'll buy you a beer if you come along with me."

Ludwig Rohne was gruff, deep-voiced, aggressive. He came into a dull afternoon, offering relief from a feeling of incompetence and Konrad welcomed that.

"I'll be glad to have a beer with you and I'll enjoy talking to you."

"I don't know whether you will or you won't, but we'll have the beer."

Ludwig Rohne led the way, turning left when they came out of the gate. "Talk will keep till we're comfortable," he said.

He was a brisk walker and his objective was nearly a mile away; a simulated stone front of miniature castle design, a swinging sign and a curving flight of steps. There were voices singing folk songs and there was a faint mist of smoke in a large rectangular room. People sat on long benches at tables equally long. There were smaller tables against the wall. Ludwig Rohne marched to one of the small tables and took it over.

"Now about my boy," he said. "I'm not certain that you're a good influence on him."

"I think I have been. I haven't hurt him."

"That remains to be seen. Some kind of a clergyman, I take it. A Monk! Not a Catholic Monk."

Konrad smiled. "That depends on what you call Catholic. I'm Russian Catholic, Russian Orthodox."

"Well, it's different and maybe the same thing. I don't

know. My wife has the religion in the family. I go along and try not to get too far out of line. What do you think of my boy Werner?"

"I like him. He has a good mind in a good body and he probably has a talent for drawing."

The waiter brought two huge steins of beer. Ludwig Rohne saluted in a perfunctory manner and drank a deep draught.

"There's where you do him no service," he said, "and maybe a hurt. Drawing will do him no good. He can make himself discontented with it."

"Maybe not."

"Maybe yes, and no maybes about it. He's a working-man's son. He can't rise much above that and no reason why he should."

"He says that you'd like him to work in the factory where you work."

"I would. It's a good place to work, a decent place. He doesn't respect what I do and he doesn't know a damned thing about it and I can't tell him anything."

"It's a razor-blade factory, isn't it?"

"Yes. So he told you that? They are good blades. Nobody makes better blades. I use them myself. Men have to have them. There's nothing to be ashamed of making them. He acts like there is."

Ludwig Rohne's attitude was belligerent, his voice loud, his manner aggressive, but Konrad discovered with surprise that he liked him.

"Werner says that you helped to build Rubble Hill," he said.

Ludwig Rohne slapped his empty stein on the table. "He told you that? I didn't know he'd bothered to think about it. Yes, I built that, helped to build it. Hell! You don't know how it was. You aren't old enough."

"I'm afraid not."

"Don't be afraid. You're damned lucky, Goddamned lucky!"

Konrad was suddenly aware that he was drinking a fresh stein of beer and that he could not remember whether it was his second or his third. Singing voices rose and fell. The place was filled with deep rhythmic sound. There was a hypnotic quality about it. Ludwig was leaning forward as he talked, a broadfaced man with a distinctive down-drooping mustache, an earnest man without any subtlety.

"This city got bombed. It got a lot of it, an awful lot of it. I wasn't here. I went up to Poland as a garrison trooper, not combat. I wasn't fit for combat after my first wound. I got that one fighting the French. Maybe I've already told you that. A man growing older becomes a Goddamned bore. I wasn't old in the army. I was seventeen when I went in and I was in battle at eighteen and I was wounded before I was nineteen. Everything moved fast. What in hell did I start to tell you?"

"About Rubble Hill."

"Yes. Got pretty far away from it, didn't I? Anyway I went to Poland, nothing much to do but wear a uniform, and I wasn't fit for much. And do you know, somebody I never saw fired out of a doorway and shot me in the leg? Well, that was pretty bad, worse than it sounds and for a while I was maybe going to lose my leg. When I could wear a uniform again they gave me light duty on the Rhine, and the Americans were bombing every night. We marched into Cologne after one of the very bad raids there and I spent a long time in Cologne."

Ludwig pounded the table with his stein and two more steins appeared. Konrad had the sensation of floating, of rising balloon-like above the table and of descending. He seemed to be anchored to the man facing him.

"You never saw a sight like Cologne," Ludwig said. "Houses, apartments, churches, everything came down. Big piles of rubble. We used to go out after a raid and try to find someone alive, or someone we could dig out. After that we collected names, tried to find out who used to live where. We made crosses and put names on them. If you saw a big heap of ruin with a cross and the name Schmidt on it, that was Schmidt's house and probably the family was there still under the debris. An apartment house heap would have maybe six or eight crosses. It was all we could do. We weren't strong enough to dig, and there was so much. We were wearing uniforms but we weren't soldiers any more, just a lot of half-sick men trying to get over our wounds. Other towns along the Rhine were like Cologne."

Ludwig Rohne's eyes were blank. He stared into space. Konrad took another swallow of the beer, surprised that he could swallow it.

"About Rubble Hill?" he said.

"Yes. That's right." Ludwig shook his shoulders. "Munich was just like Cologne and the rest of them, heaps and piles of stuff that used to be houses, stuff with white crosses on top. I was a prisoner of war, you know. Americans. I was lucky it wasn't the Russians. They worked their prisoners ten or twelve years before they let them go." He blinked. "Sorry. Shouldn't have mentioned it. You're a Russian."

"Yes. I didn't fight the war. You did."

"Right. Anyway, I might have been luckier. It was better to be captured by the British although the Americans were all right later. It makes no difference now. I came home. I was a Nazi soldier. Hell. I was a boy when I put on the uniform. What did I know about politics? I never hurt anybody who wasn't trying to hurt me, and I got my share of the hurt, but it was difficult for me to get work, to get anything. That's all over. It was a long time before me, and fellows like me, got around to cleaning up the city where we lived. We did it with volunteered time and we hauled those heaps and piles, and all that was in them, to the edge of town. We built three hills with those houses and furniture and the bones of them that owned the stuff once. The city came along after us and brought in soil from the country to cover what was there, and they planted grass in it. Those hills are there and you can climb them and if you're me, you know what's under your feet and you remember a lot of things, a lot of things."

He broke off suddenly. The music was moving into a new number and he raised his voice: *Im München steht ein Hofbrauhaus*. His voice rang through the large hall, a deep, true baritone of incredible volume. The singers close to him ceased their efforts and looked at him with respect. So, too, did Konrad. At the conclusion of the number several people called out to him and steins banged. Ludwig pushed his chair back.

"We will go," he said. "I talk too much. I bellow. I am acting like a conceited fool."

"No. You have a magnificent voice."

Konrad followed him down the aisle of tables, aware that he was lurching, unsure of his footing and of his vision. "I have a good voice, *Ja*," Ludwig said. "Not trained but good. I love music but what is that in Germany? It is all I have of culture."

They climbed the stairs and Konrad leaned against the pseudo stone wall at the top. Ludwig, too, was bracing himself, breathing heavily.

"A man should not drink in a basement," he said. "The climb up adds two drinks."

The street outside was a mere road, unpaved, slightly uneven. "I am glad to hear about my son, that he speaks of me," Ludwig said. "I have three daughters. With all those women in the house I am glad to have one son. Damn! I cannot talk to him. I can talk to you and you are a Russian. No offense! It is a thing to remark only."

"Your son is proud of you, I am sure, but he does not like the idea of the factory."

Konrad had to measure the words out, laying them down, one word at a time. Ludwig stopped in the middle of the road to listen to him.

"Men work in factories because people want things which can be made only in factories," he said. "Even my son. I do honest work. I run a good machine. It is not easy. A man must learn. It is the best I can do. I started late. The war and all that came after it! My son, perhaps, can earn more, can do more important work. I do not know. He can live in a decent home, marry, support a family. I want that for him. What is wrong with it?"

"Nothing," Konrad said.

Even with fog rolling around inside of his head he could see the other man's bewilderment, his need to be important to his son, to share things with him.

They walked along in silence, the beer catching up with them as they walked. When they reached the gateway to Streber Gardens they stood facing each other, swaying slightly.

"It has been a good thing, having this time with you," Ludwig Rohne said.

"Yes," Konrad said. "A good thing."

He made his way, with great effort, up the street to his house. He was aware of Ursula Vaclav's voice but he did not know what she was saying. He fell across the bed in his own room and a thought lived briefly in his mind. He would not be able to say his prayers tonight. On that thought he slept.

Chapter Seven

Konrad awakened early on Monday morning. He lay staring at the ceiling, aware that it was time to rise and fighting his own awareness. He had never owned a watch or a clock but he had always been able to tell, within a few minutes, what time it was, or to awaken at an hour that he set. He commented, rather proudly, on this quality of his to Father Stephen one day and the priest had snorted.

"The stupidest animal can do that," Father Stephen said. "Do not pride yourself on it."

Today he was not priding himself on anything. The morning was dark and there was a taste of decay in his mouth. His head ached. He rolled out of bed, shaved by the sense of touch and dressed mechanically. The streets were quiet and he walked two miles before stopping for a breakfast that he had difficulty in eating. The last two miles of his walk to work were a mere exercise in lifting his feet and setting them down again.

He worked all day on the Ninth Station: Jesus Falls the Third Time.

The walk home was almost as difficult as the walk down. He did not see anybody or anything en route and he did not think of anything or imagine anything. The house was fragrant, as usual, with warmth in the mingled essences and odors of cooking. He seated himself wearily and Ursula Vaclav turned her back to the stove and looked at him.

"I did not know that Monks got drunk," she said.

"A man can get drunk, forgetting that he is a Monk."

"I suppose so. What were you drinking?"

"Beer."

"That takes much practice if you want to drink a lot of it."

"I did not have the practice. Do you drink beer?"

"Very little. I prefer wine. I bought a bottle from a different vineyard for tonight."

Konrad looked at the tall bottle of wine without enthusiasm. It was a larger bottle than those they had had on other nights. It looked green with the light shining through the bottle and that was an unfortunate effect. The girl was serving food, some kind of a chicken dish similar to a fricassee. He opened the wine, working against his will because opening was expected of him. The wine was not green: it was a soft gold. To his surprise the chicken was delicious and he ate two helpings of it. To his further surprise he enjoyed the wine and drank his full share of that, feeling better than he had felt all day.

"Let us neglect the dishes," the girl said. "I have something to tell you. It would be better to sit outside."

She led the way to their minuscule porch. Konrad had to stretch his legs before him when he sat down. The girl doubled hers, hugging them, looking forward over her knees. There was a flow of dim light from the gate lantern. They could see each other as wraithlike figures, not seated closely nor companionably, withdrawn into separate worlds in more than the physical sense. The weekend people had gone home and the Gardens were quiet. There was a tree with pink blossoms which stood between them and the source of light.

"I had a letter from my mother today," the girl said. "She does not want me to come home."

"But why not? What does she expect you to do?"

"She does not say. She just does not want me to come."

Konrad stared at her. She seemed unreal, an apparition, an image of the night like the pink tree. "I do not understand," he said.

"Probably not. You would have to understand Czechoslovakia and understand my parents, either of which is impossible. Do you mind if I talk?"

"I wish that you would."

"Thank you. I need to talk or I believe that I do. That's the same thing, isn't it? I came from Kladno in Czechoslovakia. That is sugar beet country and it is not lovely. There is an ironworks and my father is a minor executive there. His name is Pavel, Pavel Vaclav. He is proud in a small way, my father. He is not richly paid but he earns more than his neighbors. He is very careful, politically, every way. He has no opinions."

"It is like that in Russia. People are careful if they possess anything."

"I have no doubt. It was always that way in Czechoslovakia, at least during my lifetime. It is worse now since the Russians are running everything. You can see why my parents are afraid to have me come home."

"No. I cannot see that."

"I have not told you enough. You know that I came here with a politician and his wife, taking care of his retarded children. He left me here. He did not go home. My parents are afraid that I would be linked to him, politically wrong where people do not dare to be wrong.

They are afraid that it would be dangerous for me to come home, dangerous for me, dangerous for them."

"Do you believe that?"

"It could be true. I would not go back to Czechoslovakia alone, without a place in the community, a family; but I would not be afraid if my family accepted me. I would then be a girl out of work, returning home. I believe that my family exaggerates danger out of their own timidity, but the danger exists."

The night was bathed in quiet. Konrad was aware of the isolation, the aloneness, that he shared with this woman. She was explaining herself to him, out of a need of her own or a belief that he needed the explanation, but the effect was one of intimacy. He had drives and urges and nights when it was a torture to seek sleep, and he knew what those things were, but he believed Father Stephen's simple statement: "That is not for us." He believed, also, in the wisdom of "Never speak to a woman, any woman, after sunset." His knowledge of women was small. Never before had he had a conversation of this length with one.

"You are your parents' daughter," he said. "If they have to take a risk for you, they should do so."

"Life is never that simple, with answers that you can put in a sentence. I do not know how to tell you the whole story but I will try. My parents believe that I shamed them, disgraced them, that their position would be injured if I were home."

"How? Why?"

"You must understand that they are simple, timid people, pious people; good Catholics, good citizens. Understand that! They are admirable. I am an only child. They sacrificed for my education. I went to college in Prague. I did not disgrace them there. I tried to live up to them. I became interested in retarded children. I discovered that I had a gift with them. I understood them and, when they did not understand anyone else, they understood me."

The girl released her knees and turned her body so that she was facing Konrad. She was rarely beautiful with the light touching her gently. Her face had a carved ivory pallor and her eyes seemed extraordinarily large.

"They hide afflicted children away so that no one has to see them," she said. "There was a school for them in Cihilka, a miserably remote place that was desperately in need of teachers. My parents did not want me to go. I felt that I had to go. There were only four of us to teach and many children to be taught and loved and cared for—"

She looked away and Konrad could see only her bowed head, hair that was black, a slender figure that seemed to shrink and to draw into itself.

"On August twenty-second, nineteen sixty-eight," she said slowly, "the Russian soldiers were in Czechoslovakia. They came to some places the day before but that is when they reached Cihilka."

She straightened, turning slowly, the light touching the ivory of her face again. Her voice was soft, level, perfectly controlled.

"They broke into our place," she said, "and I was raped many times that night by the soldiers. How many times I do not know."

The words, despite their calm delivery, were like icy water. Konrad felt the shock in them and he responded to shock, neither speaking nor reasoning. He rose abruptly and walked the few feet which separated the house from the edge of the property, to the empty street on which the light fell like running water. He stood there and the girl's words repeated themselves in his brain: "I was raped many times that night by the soldiers. How many times I do not know." He turned to go back to her and she was no longer where he had left her.

She was washing the dishes when he entered the house. He took a dishtowel and she did not protest his drying the dishes that she washed. There was a sense of horror in his mind and he did not look at her.

"Did you have a child?" he said.

"No."

"Disease?"

"No."

"Then why did your parents feel that you had disgraced them?"

"Maybe I will tell you, maybe not. Let us finish these dishes."

They worked in silence and when the dishes were put away, the girl stood in the middle of the room for a moment, neither looking at Konrad nor consciously ignoring him. She was slender and small and there was softness in her, in the way she was made and in the impression she created. There was sadness in her, too; in her face, in her full, dark eyes.

"I will try to tell you," she said.

She walked out to the porch and sat as she had before, her legs drawn up. Konrad was awkward in getting down, in finding space for his legs, aware of his body as he seldom was, of the clumsiness of it. He sensed a withdrawn quality in the girl. He had lost equality in companionship when he walked away from her.

"You should be able to understand my parents," she said. "All religious people are alike. Sex is sinful to them even if it is something that is thrust upon one. The good God-fearing people of Cihilka did not do one damned thing for us, and we were teachers in their school. They made us get right out of town after the attack so we wouldn't

cause trouble for them with the Russians. We needed
hospital treatment and we had to go to Prague for it. We
went there in a truck. A truck! The people of Cihilka
treated us like prostitutes."

"It is difficult to believe."

She turned swiftly and there was fire in her, a fury of
tightened fists and clenched teeth. "It shouldn't be," she
said. "Not difficult to believe at all. That is how *you*
treated me when I told you what happened to me. That
is how my family treated me. I had lost caste. I was a
fallen woman."

"No."

"Yes."

"I thought no such thing. I was shocked at what had
happened to you."

"And disgusted."

"No."

He thrust his hand out in protest and his fingers touched
her forearm. Her skin was soft and warm to his touch. She
raised her eyes to his and the combat went out of her. She
drew her arm away.

"Well, whatever you felt or feel," she said huskily, "you
know the story of my life now, the good and the bad of
it. I am on your charity until I find an answer to my
problem and I can't help it."

"There is no charity."

"Of course there is. I'm here. The Germans won't let
me stay a minute once they see my papers. Without my
family's help I cannot go back to Czechoslovakia. No
matter how innocent I was, I was with a man who escaped
from the Russian government."

Konrad stared out into the darkness. He felt very close
to this woman, closer than he would have believed possible,

close in sympathy, in the sharing of her problem. She was looking into his face.

"What can I do?" she said.

He shook his head. "I don't know."

"Neither do I." She rose, standing for a poised moment while he struggled to his feet. "You have been patient listening to me. I was a bore but there was relief in talking. So much has been bottled up, so very much." She waved her hand. "I'll work things out, some way. Good night."

She was gone before he had a chance to assure her that she was not a bore, that she had involved him in her story, that he wanted desperately to help her. He made an impatient brushing gesture with his right hand. Telling her all of that would be spouting empty rhetoric, solving nothing, offering only words when she had words enough of her own.

He walked again to the street which bisected the Gardens. All of the houses were dark tonight and nothing stirred. There were stars, and the light by the gate; nothing else. He was the only creature on Earth. Or, no! He and the girl were the only creatures on Earth, the two of them.

He was restless with awareness of the woman. He was outraged at what had happened to her. He was a Russian and, in a sense, shared the guilt of his countrymen. He could understand the girl hating him. He was a symbol of "them."

His restlessness he considered absurd, a blinding of instinct and silence and the night. He knew nothing of women. He had sat with another woman one night in Vienna and he had been even more helpless than he had been tonight. She had been a prostitute. He tried to erase that memory as swiftly as it came. Ursula Vaclav said that he considered her a prostitute because she had been raped.

He did not, and he did not mean to link her in memory with the girl in Vienna. There were so few women in his life to remember.

Deslys? He could see her again, coming out on that stage in Vienna, with all the laughter and the happiness that she brought to it. He could hear again the little tinkling bells in her voice when she sang and see the small gestures that she made with her hands.

He walked back and forth, remembering. There would never be another Deslys. There was nothing in Ursula Vaclav that even reminded him of Deslys.

Weariness wrapped him and he looked up at the stars. He had missed his hour of prayer last night and he would miss it again tonight. There was nothing in himself to offer. He was a spiritual blank.

Chapter Eight

There was a note from the Mother Superior on Konrad's work bench in the morning, requesting him to report to her office at ten o'clock. He did a mental run-through of his days in the convent without finding any derelictions and patiently waited out the time. He had no watch so he was five minutes early for the appointment. The Mother Superior sat behind her desk, coldly beautiful, with no light in her eyes.

"Sister Agathe has brought me a few objects that were hidden away for a long time," she said. "They seem to be in rather bad condition. I wonder if there is anything that you can do to restore them."

She rose and crossed the room to a long table against the wall. There were a number of pieces of bronze statuary. They were encrusted, corroded, dirty. There was a Madonna with green spots. He studied a two figure piece, an annunciation scene, which was the best in the group. He lifted a group of three singing angels, turned it in his hand and laid it down. It had a green and gray surface with streaks of bronze.

"That is plaster," he said, "shellacked and varnished by someone who knew what he was doing. I could make it convincingly bronze again."

There was a slight change of expression in the nun's face and he knew that she was aware of this plaster among the genuine bronzes. The Madonna had bronze disease and would have to be handled carefully. The annunciation scene required even gentler care or it could, conceivably, crumple.

"They can, I believe, be restored," he said, "but it will take time and patience."

"And skill. Can you do it?"

"Yes. Not in that workroom downstairs. Do you have a laboratory?"

"Yes."

"I would use that. I have instruments and compounds of my own at home, but not perfect for this. I would like some new things."

"What?"

"Caustic soda, sodium, sesquicarbonate, acetic acid, a few other things. Some needles and small chisels, metal handles for the needles, scrapers, brushes." He spread his hands apart. "That is, ideally. I can do with less. I could use a secondhand dental drill, jeweler's hammer, an etcher's needle."

The nun's eyes were intent now, fixed upon his face. "Do you know where to buy these things?"

"No. I would look for shops near the university."

"Take the day off and find them." She reached in her desk drawer and brought out one of the familiar envelopes which carried his daily pay. She opened another drawer and withdrew a sheaf of currency. She seemed to be doing mental arithmetic with the money in her hand. She counted out several bills then and handed them to him.

"This should do it. A little over, I believe. I will want receipts for what you spend. There is less money here than you, perhaps, imagine, and I am accountable."

He nodded. "I'll buy carefully."

It was a strange sensation, walking out into the city's morning with money in his pockets and a shopping project outlined. He had never shopped for anything except the food that he and Stephen had eaten in Vienna, a few other things equally simple. The proprietors of his shops, when he found them, discovered that he knew what he wanted, that he knew all of the tools, glues, solvents, and chemicals of the restorer's art, and the substitutes that would work when first choices were not available.

He had made all of his purchases by two-thirty and he left them in care of the last shopkeeper, to be picked up in the morning; a bulky package. The day was now his own and he decided to survey neighborhoods close to the convent as possible living space. He could not live indefinitely at Streber Gardens and when he no longer had to consider Ursula Vaclav's need, a shorter walk to work would be desirable.

He followed a rambling route into a neighborhood he had never seen before, dwellings of all sizes and shapes which fitted into an arc, the streets curving. This small sector, obviously, had escaped the bombing or was lightly hit. The houses were old.

There was a tall, shabby apartment building with a plaque on the wall beside the door. The inscription stated that Vladimir Ilyich Ulyanov Lenin had lived in this building in 1901 and 1902. Konrad stood staring at the plaque. He knew little history but he knew of Lenin, the father of the Russian revolution. One could not be a Russian and be ignorant of him. He had lived in this building, Lenin, a long time ago. Other people lived now in the rooms which had been his, poor people. The neighborhood had been, no doubt, a center of poverty when Lenin knew it, and it was still that kind of a neighborhood.

A short distance from Lenin's shrine there was a Roman Catholic church. Konrad stopped to look at it. It was a poor man's church; a structure with a steeple and white pillars in the front, a Byzantine dome at the rear. It was the church of St. Ursula.

"Ursula! I'll have to tell her that she has a church in Munich. She won't care but it is interesting."

He did not know the saint, knew nothing about her, but he thought of the girl on the way home. She was obviously not a religious girl and he wondered why, but the reason, whatever it was, belonged in her private life, something between herself and God.

When he reached home, Ursula Vaclav was not there. Streber Gardens had a deserted look and his own house appeared deserted like the rest. He walked through to the kitchen and he knew, then, why Ursula was not home. He was early. This was her shopping time. He felt weary and it would have been pleasant to sit quietly and wait for her, but he suddenly remembered Otto. The boy had given him a card with his address on it and he had never called on him. It was a thing to do.

He took the card from his pocket and looked at it. Otto's name was on it, Otto Genzelt. It was not a pleasant name. There was certainly no music in it. One had a difficult time finding anything attractive in Otto, or about Otto, yet there was something there, something appealing under all of the harsh, displeasing qualities that one saw.

The weather was changing and Konrad looked at the clouds with a wary eye. They had been heavy, motionless, breeders of a dull day all afternoon, but now they were in motion, driven by some high altitude wind. A man could be hit with heavy rain as a reward for walking away from the shelter of home.

The Genzelt house was one of a precise square of houses

a short distance beyond the Lagerhaus where Otto worked in the summer. Otto opened the door. He had a scrubbing brush in his hand and there was a pail of sudsy water standing in midroom. A carpet had been rolled back. Otto was obviously embarrassed. He made an apologetic gesture.

"She wants the floor scrubbed once a week," he said. "This is the day I do it."

"On your hands and knees?"

"That's the way she wants it done."

Konrad walked around the edge of the scrubbing area to a small dining room that opened off the parlor space.

"Do you mind if I finish?" Otto said.

"Go right ahead."

Konrad seated himself on a stiff, hard chair. All of the furniture in the house was of mass-production design, angular and without any pretense of beauty. He watched Otto at work. The boy was an expert with a scrubbing brush. There was long practice behind his technique. He did not slop the water on; he used a little at a time, drying as he went along. He finished the room and took the chair which faced Konrad's.

"I didn't think you would come," he said.

"Why not? I'm a friend of yours."

Otto looked away. "I wasn't sure."

"Why not?"

"I don't have friends."

"You should have. You were a friend to me when I needed one." Konrad thought of Werner's remark that Otto did not want to be what he was afraid that he was. "Do you do all the housework around here, Otto?" he said.

"Most of it. My mother works."

"And you go to school. What does your mother do?"

"She is a saleslady in a store."

"You do the cooking, too."

"Who told you?"

"I wondered. You made that soup that you brought me for the girl, didn't you? Your mother didn't have anything to do with it?"

Otto's eyes shifted. "It was soup that we had around. I thought maybe you'd need it."

"I did. Nobody else thought about me at all. That's why I'm your friend."

"Thanks."

Otto was far more assured in his own home, a long way from the boy who made an entire conversation out of the term "son of a bitch," but he was still vague, a youth with a weak mouth and slack in his jaw. He lacked Werner's assurance, Werner's physique, Werner's well-fed look; but there was something, something elusive that Otto had and that Werner did not have.

"Tell me, Otto," Konrad said. "You were embarrassed when I came while you were scrubbing that floor. Why?"

"I don't know. It's a woman's work. A lot of what I do is woman stuff."

"Maybe not. It's just work that is waiting for someone to do it. I grew up in a monastery. We, each, did our share of the work. We were males. We had no females in the place. We cooked and scrubbed and cleaned and did laundry. We weren't sissies. We were Monks. Some of us were pretty tough."

Otto's eyes were intent now, not shifting. "I've never seen a monastery," he said. "I don't know how they work."

"I'll tell you some time. For now, what would you like to do? As a career, a job, a way to make a living? *Quick!*"

"Drive a truck, a big truck."

"Why?"

"I would love to travel, to have one of those big things

to handle. I'd like to see new places, a lot of people, not stay in one place."

"You'd have to have the one place, too. You wouldn't be traveling all the time."

"No. I'd come back to it. That would be home, but I'd travel and I'd be doing work I liked to do."

"Any reason why you can't when you're older, when you're out of school?"

"My mother hates the idea. She won't even discuss it."

"What does she want you to do?"

"Work in a bank. Or a store. Do something where I'd be dressed up every day."

"We can't all do that." Konrad rose. "Finish school, Otto," he said. "Keep your truck dream if that's what you want. Nobody will keep you from it if you really want it."

"You believe that?"

"Certainly. I'll have to go along now. We will have other talks. If you come to my place on a weekend you won't need a key. The gate is open."

"Is that woman still there?"

"Her name is Ursula Vaclav. She is."

"Oh," Otto looked away. His eyes came quickly back. "When were you born?"

"What has that got to do with anything?"

"Nothing. I'd like to know. Month and date."

Konrad shrugged. He had never been certain that he knew the date of his birth or, for that matter, his name. He knew what was written on his papers.

"September 17, 1944," he said.

"Virgo. That's a good sign. When was the woman born?"

"I haven't the slightest idea. What difference does it make?"

"My mother could tell you all about yourself, just knowing when you were born. She is an astrologer. That's why she is late tonight. She is at a meeting."

Konrad laughed. "They never taught anything like that in the monastery," he said.

"They should. It's important. I'm an Aquarian."

There was a sudden clap of thunder that shook the frail house. "My stars are telling me to go home," Konrad said. "I've had a good time. See you later."

He plunged out into the rain. He had not exaggerated in saying that he had had a good time. The visit had been a duty chore but he had found it fascinating. No one would ever see on the surface the potential of Otto. The world needed truck drivers, many of them. Why shouldn't he be one?

The rain was coming gently but the speed and the volume increased as he ran toward home. The thunder, too, increased. The sound seemed to roll around the sky, touching all points of the compass. Lightning slashed through it. It was a black night when the lightning wasn't playing. Konrad realized that he had stayed longer at Otto's than he had planned. Ursula would be home and wondering about him.

He covered the last two hundred yards at a sprint, with the rain an almost solid wall about him. He was wet, so wet that he could feel the water on his skin under his clothing, or through his clothing, icily cold. There was no light at the gate of Streber Gardens and no light in his house. He stumbled through the tool room door as the rolling thunder made another clamourous circle, with the lightning flashing three times.

Ursula, crouched on the kitchen floor, screamed.

Konrad saw the girl clearly in the brilliant light. There was terror in her face. He went down on one knee beside her and she gripped his right forearm with both hands.

"I am so glad you came," she said. "I'm afraid of storms. I cannot stand—oh!"

Thunder shook the house again and he put his arm around her protectively as she turned in to him. He was aware of such an irrelevance as the fact that he was very wet, that water trickled off his clothing onto the floor, that the girl would be as wet as he was if she stayed close to him.

"I'm afraid," she said. "I can't help it. I'm afraid."

"Don't be. You'll be all right. Nothing will hurt you."

Thunder cannonaded again and the lightning seemed, for a second, to be in the room with them. The girl gripped him tightly and he sat on the floor beside her, holding her inside the circle of his arm. She was soft and frightened and very small. Her body was trembling and she clung to him, her face buried in the curve of his shoulder.

"It will be all over in a few minutes," he said. "This kind of storm never lasts long."

He was surprised that his voice trembled. He was aware of the girl now in all of his body, the nearness of her, her dependence upon him, their complete isolation from a riotously noisy world.

"I will not let anything happen to you," he said.

He felt the tightening of the girl's grip and he listened, appalled, to the echo of his own words. He had never said anything sillier. He was promising to protect her from lightning. He did not have to promise her anything.

The thunder rumbled in the distance and if there was lightning accompanying it, the lightning was distant, too. He held the girl close and he liked holding her, liked her trust in himself, her dependence. It was quiet now save for the sound of the falling rain, a sound he had always liked.

"My favorite cell in the monastery was a wonderful place

to hear rain," he said. "I would go to sleep hearing it, trying to stay awake."

"How long were you in the monastery?"

Her voice came up to him. He looked into the darkness of the kitchen. He could, often, see more in darkness than in light.

"Nearly all of my life," he said. "I cannot remember the first years. I was so very small."

"Was there anyone to take care of you except men?"

"In the monastery? No. We didn't need anybody but men."

"You did, but you didn't know it." She shook her shoulders and freed herself from his encircling arm. "I have been a fool again, at my worst. I am ashamed. I couldn't help it."

She gained her feet with a swift, flowing motion. Konrad was less graceful, slower. She stood facing him. "You were very good to me," she said. "Patient. And you are soaking wet. Change your clothes and perhaps I will have light by then so that I can fix your supper."

He had little interest in supper. He did not want to leave the girl. The Monk inside the man derided him and he knew that the Monk was justified.

"You are wet yourself," he said.

She laughed. "Contagion. I was not out in the rain. I, too, will change."

She went to her own room before he went to his. He was aware of her in all of his nerve system as he changed clothes. He did not have variety in clothing. He vetoed the idea of wearing his Monk's robe and settled, because he had no alternative, for his stained and worn work pants, his gray shirt.

There was no light. He had not anticipated a blackout, and neither had the girl. There were no candles. He groped his way back to the kitchen and almost collided with Ursula. He had a swift passing mental note that he thought of her as "Ursula" now where he had always thought of her as "Ursula Vaclav." That change had occurred before the storm, somewhere on his walk of the afternoon, probably after he had seen the church with her name on it.

"I cannot cook anything," she said, "but I can make sandwiches."

"I'll help you."

"You can open the wine."

His eyes had adjusted to the darkness and he could see fairly well. Ursula was wearing her striped blouse and a dark skirt. She handed him a bottle of the white wine. She had chilled it. Sometimes she did and sometimes she served it at room temperature. It was good either way.

They sat at the table with their sliced meat and their bread. Some restraint had slipped away from them. They were, for the first time, friends, Konrad thought. He had never heard Ursula laugh until tonight. She had a soft laugh with music in it.

"I discovered today that I am a Virgo," he said. "I knew only vaguely that there was such a thing."

"Who told you?"

"A boy named Otto. His mother is an astro-ologist, or whatever they call them."

"I could have told you. I am a Libra, born October 11. Astrology is interesting. I like dreams better. Do you have a favorite dream?"

"I do not know whether it is a favorite or not. There was a stairway at the monastery that frightened me when I was small. Day or night it frightened me. Sometimes in dreams it comes back."

"What was it like?"

"It was at the end of a long corridor that connected two buildings. It went up on a long slant, straight. I could see the top of it, an arch with darkness behind it. There were sixty steps and there was a plain, flat-surface barrow path two feet wide paralleling the steps. Carts or cases, a variety of things, could be hauled up or sent down on that. It was a kind of open chute. I was a messenger when I was very young and I had to climb all those steps with messages. I always expected to see somebody or *something* come out of the darkness and through the arch. In dreams I still do."

"And nobody ever did?"

"While I was climbing the stairs? No. If anyone ever did, I'd remember him and not the fear of the unknown. I wouldn't dream."

"You might. I have a dream, too. I cannot explain it as clearly as you explain yours. It doesn't seem to mean anything but it is a vivid dream and I have it often. I had it when I was a small girl."

"What is it?"

"It is a door, a house door, quite ordinary but pleasant in appearance. It is in a frame, a regular frame, but the frame is not attached to anything. It stands out in the middle of a big field, the kind of field we have in Czechoslovakia in the flatlands. The frame is always black or dark brown, but sometimes the door is red or yellow or green or brown. It is standing open, partly open, and I am walking across the field to it. I am walking to that door with the intention of entering it, or whatever one does to a door that is not attached to anything; but I never quite do it. I can look through the open door to the emptiness beyond and I can see every detail of the door, but that is as far as I can go. I never step through."

The girl had said that it was a vivid dream and she made

it vivid in the telling. The room was dark, black dark, but he could see her. She was leaning forward against the table, very solemn and intent. She was a brunette study but she had lovely teeth, very white teeth. They would appear large if her mouth was not wide.

"There does not seem any point in going through your door if there is nothing on the other side," he said.

"Maybe. Maybe not. Didn't you ever want to do something that you knew, instinctively, was not worth doing?"

"I don't know. I would have to think about that."

"Think about it while we do the dishes."

She rose and he accompanied her. There was mystery in the darkness, a sense of being in the power of something that he could not control. Light or no light depended upon some force outside and beyond himself, some force that he could not locate or imagine. He did not know where electricity was made in Munich, or generated if that was the term, and he did not know how it was made. He passed dishes to Ursula and there was companionship in the passing as there had been companionship in conversation at a table, the sharing of dreams. She was a form beside him, moving into deeper shadow out of absolute darkness, if that was possible, and moving back again.

She did not speak and he was locked in a strange silence himself, aware of every move that the woman made, warned from some depth within himself that he should not be aware yet beyond the touch of the warning.

He dried the last dish and handed it to her. She put it away, stretching above herself to put it away, and turning slightly toward him as she came down from her tiptoes. He stepped toward her and she was in his arms. He held her gently then pressed her harder against himself. Her voice came up to him.

"Oh, no. Not now. I don't think so—"

Her face rose to his and he kissed her. He had never kissed a woman and the warmth of her flowed into him, bringing a strange excitement with it, a blinding want of repetition. He held her momentarily away from him then swept her back again.

"You can't . . ." she said.

He wanted her, wanted all of her. He swept her up in his arms and held her, free of the floor, free of all other contact save that with himself. Her arm went around his neck and he walked with her into her own room.

He lost all sense of detail. He was in a raging storm and the girl was not fighting him, not opposing him. She clung to him and then her hands moved on his body as his moved on hers. He kissed her and his whole being seemed to explode, to expand out beyond his consciousness into some occult area of joy and pain and blinding light.

He talked to the girl and he called her Ursula but he did not know what he said nor what she said in reply. They lay, at length, locked in each other's arms and wrapped in a great peace, floating in a bottomless cavern of sensation, knowing that they would move again into ecstasy but not yet. He passed his hand over her hair.

"I didn't know what it was like," he said.

"Wasn't there ever another woman?"

"No. Oh, no. I didn't even speak to women except where I worked."

"I'm glad," she said.

"I had no right to do this to you."

"Do what? We did it. Whatever! We did it together."

"I hope so. I feel selfish."

"Do not be. You shouldn't be. Believe me, you should not be."

She raised her head and he kissed her again. Beyond that point there was no reasoning and no blame, no sense of right or wrong.

Chapter Nine

Ursula was asleep when Konrad rose in the morning. He stood beside the bed, looking down at her. She slept beautifully, her head turned slightly to the right, her left hand with fingers curled resting on the covers. She looked young, very young, and the skin of her face was smooth, clear, without color. She had heavy black lines on her eyebrows, the only artificial touch. Konrad shook his head. It was incredible that this girl was in his life and he in hers; unbelievable.

He moved softly in shaving, dressing, leaving the house. It was early and the morning was light gray. There was no rain, no threat of rain. He had had less sleep than he normally had but he was only moderately tired and the weariness worked off in the first two miles of walking, the stop for breakfast.

It was astonishing that everything seemed as it had been on other mornings. He had passed through a tremendous experience and his life was changed forever but no one noticed any difference in him. He paused briefly before the statue of the Sacred Heart in the lower hall of the convent. It was Roman Catholic art and he had never cared for it, but he respected the symbology. This was the Lord, Jesus

Christ, standing with his heart exposed, his hands inviting the sinner to come to Him. Certainly, if no one else noticed a change in him, Konrad thought, God would know. There had not been, and was not now, any sign from God. He was alone in his own knowledge of himself.

He had picked up his bundle at the shop and at 9:15 Sister Agathe came to the laboratory to look at it. She was an old woman with a face that was a contour map, wrinkled, laid in a pattern of elevations and depressions, of loops and curving lines. She seemed less interested in his purchases than in the cost of them. He gave her the receipts and the change from the Mother Superior's money. She went away happy and he was alone again, disinclined to cope with bronzes and more in a mood for wood. He returned to work on the Stations of the Cross and the day passed swiftly.

He walked eagerly in going home. He had experienced a feeling of guilt through the day, a consciousness of sin, but there had been a strange unreality in the thought of sin and guilt in connection with Ursula. The thought dropped away from him as he walked and then returned in another form as he neared his house. He did not know how the day had dealt with the girl, how she might think or feel. She might believe that he had taken advantage of the fact that she had nowhere to go, no escape from him. She had told him several times that she hated him. She might be hating him again.

There was a fragrance of cooking vegetables in the kitchen. Ursula was standing beside the stove and she turned swiftly when he entered. She had a smile that he had never seen before, a smile that started in her eyes and curved across her lips. There was happiness in her.

"I have two trout," she said. "They are very cheap."

"They should be. If you weren't lazy you could go

back to that shack in the clearing and catch all the trout you wanted in the stream behind the trees."

"So! Did you catch any?"

"I thought about it."

It seemed the most natural thing in the world to walk across the kitchen floor and kiss her. She kissed him in return, then pushed him away, good-naturedly but firmly.

"Entertain me while I work," she said.

"I have no gifts for entertainment."

He sat in a chair and looked at her. The Monk inside of him was startled and upset, unable to fit this kitchen and this girl into a tightly knit pattern of more than twenty years. The man in the chair was aware of the Monk but his life in this moment was here, rich in satisfaction, in promise, in a strange excitement that moved under his skin.

Ursula was wearing a blouse that he had not seen before. It was maroon, a color that enriched her own dark beauty. She wore an apron over blouse and skirt, a white apron with a pattern of thin red lines in it. She talked as she worked at the stove, letting the words float back over her shoulder.

"I liked hearing about your long stairs and the arch," she said. "I kept seeing it in my mind all day. I never saw a Russian monastery. Tell me more about yours."

"You would find it dull. It was a place of Monks. Nothing for women."

"What did it look like?"

He thought to himself that the answer was obvious. It looked like a monastery and could look like nothing else; but that was frivolous. All monasteries did not look alike. Each had its own design, its own setting, its own personality.

"It was huge," he said. "A man walked miles, walking around it. It had many onion-shaped domes, six of them blue and four gold. The main church was bigger than most cathedrals and it had a tall thin tower with bells in it. Once upon a time thousands of people came."

He broke off suddenly, aware of the girl's eyes. She was afraid, as he was. She wanted to talk or to keep him talking. It was one thing to be picked up in a storm and swept out of oneself, another thing to sit at the table with the person who had shared that storm. He extended his hand, laying it over hers on the tabletop.

"Last night," he said, "I loved you more than anyone in the world."

She drew her hand away. "It is nice to know that, to know that for one night, one was loved."

"It was not merely for one night."

"It was, of course. You could not love me. I am a series of ugly pictures in your mind, horrid pictures."

"No."

She rose and walked away from the table. She walked into the yard and he followed her. He would have put his arm around her but she blocked him, her fingers tightening over his. They stood together looking out at the dark houses of their neighbors. The light at the gate was shining tonight. There were blossoms between them and the light, either invincible blossoms proof against rain or blossoms freshly opened since the storm.

"Is this where you pray?" she said.

"No. Back farther, close to the house."

"Strange," she said. "It is natural, perhaps for a Monk, or seems natural, but praying is like talking to yourself. There is no one there."

"There is God."

"A myth of men. I don't believe women would have invented God. Men did that and women went along."

"Men didn't invent the stars which keep perfect time or

the minds that can read stars or the great wonder and variety of growing things, Ursula," he said.

"They happened. They evolved."

"Out of nothing, from nothing." He laughed. "Come with me when I pray at night. Do not pray if you do not believe. Merely recite to yourself all the reasons why you do not believe that there is a God. Do that every night for a week. At the end of the week you will have fewer reasons than you had at the beginning; perhaps no reasons at all."

"No! What do you do when you pray, think of all the reasons why you believe that there *is* a God?"

"I don't have to do that."

He looked out into space. It was very difficult to even attempt an explanation, or a description, of what he did in prayer. He tried, telling her how it was, the sense of Presence, the projection of himself out of his body, the thoughts or memories or images that came unbidden.

"It is like telepathy," she said.

"I don't know."

"It is. I do not know with whom you are communicating. You project thought. There seems to be something that sends it back."

"That sounds unnecessarily complicated."

"It isn't. Not really. Animals communicate without words, projecting thought. So do retarded children, some of them. Few people realize that. I can talk to some children without saying a word and they do what I tell them to do."

"You're sure that you aren't deceiving yourself?"

"Positive. I am a teacher. I have to know how to communicate or I am nothing."

Konrad lifted the fingers entwined in his own and looked at them. It was astonishing to have a conversation like this, and with a woman. They had to talk, of course. They were people who did not know each other and they were very close. They were standing outside themselves, talking, aware of the forces coiled within them, aware that the forces would move again.

"I am certain that people talked to one another once without words," the girl said, "and that people will do it again some day. I believe that animals are baffled, astonished at us, that we cannot do it."

She was so serious, solemn serious, not looking at him; looking, as he so often did himself, at something out and beyond the place where she was.

"Words satisfy me," he said. "I love you. I love your voice and watching your face when you speak, holding your hand."

"Merely because I am a woman. You are a man. You are supposed to feel that way about a woman. I am the only woman you know."

"You are enough."

He looked into her eyes and he watched her, wanted her beyond the enduring. She moved toward him slightly, or seemed to move, and he swept her into his arms. After the first moment of startled struggle her body went limp. Her hand moved up his back between his shoulder blades and her lips met his. The storm picked them up then and carried them.

They lay quietly in each other's arms after a long while. Her head was below his, her hair against his cheek. "You are not merely a woman," he said. "You are all women. There cannot be anything else like you."

"It would be nice to believe that."

"I have heard of men being in love, and read about them and I did not understand. Now I know."

"You are sweet, and very young. It is hard to believe." Her hand stroked his face. "How old are you?"

"I was born in 1944."

"Twenty-five. I am twenty, and I am much older than you are."

Twenty! He thought about that. He had not thought of Ursula in terms of age, had never phrased a thought about age in connection with her. He was surprised now that she was only twenty, yet not surprised. So much about her was young and vulnerable. He had a flash of thought about those men, those soldiers of Russia, hurting her and he could not endure it. He banished the thought in almost the moment that it came, but its echoes ran in his brain.

"Ursula," he said. "I am not a thief. I would like to give as well as take."

"You do give. You have no idea how much."

"Not enough. I have very little to offer you. I have never needed much, so I do not have what I didn't seek. You will need things. I will try to get them for you." He drew a deep breath. "I am not a priest, Ursula. I have no vows. There is no barrier. Will you share what I have, marry me?"

She turned in his arms, facing him. It was dark in the room but she was nude, as he was. "Are you proposing to me?" she said. "You are, aren't you?"

"Call it that. Call it anything. I want to spend my life with you."

She threw her arms around him, her head against his chest. "You are sweet, so very sweet." Her voice caught, halfway between laughter and tears. "Did any other man in the history of the world ever ask a woman to marry him in such a situation as this?"

"That is irrelevant. Will you?"

"I can't. I can't. But, Konrad, I will remember this moment all of my life."

"Why can't you?"

"You forget. You forget, darling, and that is lovely. I would rather have you remember me and forget facts. Marriages take licenses and records and priests or ministers —and your dear Germans would not marry us. They would send me back to Czechoslovakia immediately."

He stared into her face, a pretty, piquant face, very white in the darkness, into her eyes which seemed enormous. He had forgotten or he had suppressed in his mind what he did not wish to remember.

"There must be a way."

"No. There are other reasons. No matter. We have what we have. I wrote to my friend today, Annchen, who had the school for the retarded children. She went back to Cihilka, the only one of us who did. When I hear from her, I, too, will go back. The government of my country will approve that. I will have no trouble."

"Why? Why should you go back?"

"Because, my dear, there is only one thing in my life that I do well. Maybe I was born to do it."

"I need you as much as the school."

"As much as the children?"

He hesitated. "Yes," he said.

"You will forget," she said. "You will find somebody else. I will hate it but I had you first, before any other woman. Nobody else will be your first, my Konrad, and sometimes you will remember me."

He had no answers for her but he had a great blind need of her and a desperate necessity for holding her to him, sharing all things, the risks with the rest.

He held her tightly, frightened by even the thought of separation, and the storm broke again, wiping out all thought.

Chapter Ten

The mind of a Monk marches on straight lines or, at the very least, on what it considers straight lines. The minds of lovers do not march; they leap and dance, swing madly to music unheard by others and settle upon no thought for long save the thought of each other. A Monk in love is, to express an idea banally, a creature of two co-existent worlds.

A four-mile walk lends itself admirably to the settling of mental confusion, the clearing of concepts, the definition of terms. A mind has no work to do on a four-mile walk unless it turns to the clearing of its own accumulated clutter or unless the possessor of the mind turns it to some task. Konrad, walking to work, was sleepy and not attracted to mental challenges. For the most part he walked with images that moved, disappeared, reappeared, changed; all images of Ursula. His mornings, too, were filled with simple discoveries. He was surprisingly in tune with people whom he did not normally see. Life sparkled with new meanings, new emphases.

German housewives hung the mattresses and bedding over the sills of upstairs windows in the early morning, half in and half out. He had been aware of the custom but it had been an awareness without seeing. He had not linked human beings to it, people who slept in houses and ate in houses and, necessarily, did housework. He was such a person now himself, to his occasional astonishment, and however distantly he shared the activity of other people, the sharing was established. He was part of the world as he had never been part before, belonging to it and to its realities, the great and the small, the meaningful and the absurd.

The Monk inside of him walked the streets that he did, walked them grimly. "Is there any good for you or for any man in what you are doing?" his Monk-self asked. "You had what few men possess and you have traded it for the toys of the mob, the commonalities of all men."

Inevitably, when the Monk within him spoke, he thought of Father Stephen. He had never known Father Stephen to be wrong about anything, or mistaken, or in doubt; but he did not believe that Father Stephen would be of help to him now. Father Stephen would disapprove of Ursula utterly, would wave her out of his life, would state without allowing an inch for compromise that sin is sin and that no amount of rationalizing ever made it anything else.

It wasn't that simple, even if the simplicity wore the garment of truth.

Ursula was not the enemy of virtue, to be banished by the virtuous. It was not a sin in Ursula that she had a woman's body. She would be his wife if they had the options possessed by the simplest peasants in a village. Ursula brought much to living, so very much that Konrad had never known. She tried, without laying emphasis on the trying, to understand the realities of his life, realities alien to her own.

Ursula sat quietly beside him during his nightly hour of prayer. She did not speak during the hour nor speak of it when the hour was over. He did not know if she experienced anything at all save the sharing, the companionship of silence. He could not, of course, ask her and he could not tell her of his own desperation. The living presence of God, or of God's messenger, was no longer there when he prayed. No visions had come to him in over a week, no scenes out of memory. He felt abandoned, outcast, divided by a gulf of guilt from all that had made his life, all that gave his life meaning.

Such moods came to him, went away, returned. The mood was blackest on a heavy, overcast Tuesday morning. The Monk within him was savagely triumphant.

"She will leave you when her letter comes," the Monk said. "She will return to Czechoslovakia and you will never see her again. What difference? You lived long years without the woman and how long, precisely, have you known her?"

He brushed the inner voice aside. He had finished his walk. The service gate of the convent loomed up before him and he passed through it, leaving the world outside.

He reached the workroom without seeing anyone. He looked with distaste at the bronze of three angels on which he had worked yesterday. There was other work to be done, an alternative, and he was grateful for that. He took the small handtruck which was part of the general basement equipment and ascended to the chapel. There were three nuns praying, each in a separate pew. He could hear sounds of movement from the sacristy. There was probably a priest vesting for a Mass or removing his vestments after saying a Mass. One way or another, it was out of the pattern of his life in this convent. He was not expected to attend Masses.

His work on the Stations of the Cross had gone well until the Mother Superior confronted him with the bronzes. He felt in tune with the Stations today, out of tune with angels.

He walked slowly down the side aisle as a man would walk who was trying to make up his mind. He knew, however, which Station he would select for his working project today. He stopped and took it reverently from the wall. It was the Twelfth Station, Jesus Dies on the Cross.

There were other nuns filing in to the chapel, a few students. He wheeled the Station out and, in the corridor, encountered the Mother Superior. She was flanked by two nuns and she stopped when she saw him, her eyes passing over the Station, lifting to his face.

"You have not finished the bronzes," she said. "I have been waiting to show you some silver."

Antagonism moved in him, strangely, inexplicably. "I did not feel like bronze today," he said. "I will work in wood."

Her eyes were cold, as they had always been cold, and she did not change expression. "Indeed?" she said. "Well, we must, perhaps, expect some temperament. Be certain that you feel like bronzes tomorrow."

She swept on and he pushed his load along the corridor to the elevator, aware of her still when she was no longer in sight. It was, he thought, illogical and unreasonable of him that he disliked the Mother Superior. She was a good employer who paid him well, provided good working conditions and everything within reason that he needed. She made no unjust demands and imposed no unfair conditions. She made no intrusion upon his private life and no inquiry as to his religious practices. Yet he, who rarely disliked anyone, disliked her.

It was, perhaps, some primitive resentment of the employed against the employer. He had encountered it in others when he worked in Vienna. His experience was limited; such resentment might be widespread.

Thinking about his resentments and dislikes seemed to dissipate them. He remembered Father Stephen standing magnificently tall one day when he criticized someone. "You are not called upon to approve them or to disapprove of them," Father Stephen said. "There is only one rule for dealing with strangers. You respect what they respect, value what they value, ignore that which pleases them if it displeases you. They are not, you must realize, compelled to be as you are."

He did not have Father Stephen with him now and this day had started badly. He lifted the Station to his workbench. With a box propped under it he could view it on an angle. This was a solemn Station, a tragic moment in time, *the* most tragic moment. Jesus Christ, incarnate God, hung dead upon the cross, the victim of man's will to sin.

The sense of his own sinfulness, his indulgent yielding to his flesh, was strong in Konrad as he stared at the grimly punished figure bowed in death.

The carver who had done this figure had been a German, a German who had followed the harsh, realistic pattern of Grunewald. This was not pretty church art, cleaned up for gentle eyes; this was an artist's portrait of death. The Saviour's body hung heavily on the hands through which nails had been driven and the bowed head bore a crown of thorns matted with blood. The bicep and forearm muscles were stretched and ropy. There were long stripes on the legs and on the torso where the rods of the floggers had fallen and there was a jagged wound on the left breast where the lance of the soldier had been thrust.

Looking at the figure on the cross, Konrad could hear again, as he had heard them so often, the voices of the

Monks chanting through the three sorrowful hours of Good Friday. His nerves ran like small reptiles under his skin, remembering them. The men who chanted had shared in the dying and Konrad, listening to them in his mind, shared the beating, the nailing, the thrust of the spear point. There was no escape from his sense of personal guilt.

The Twelfth Station, for some reason, had been damaged less than any of the fourteen, affected less by deteriorating forces. Konrad washed it and worked wax into a break on the left arm of the cross, into a crack in the right leg of the crucified figure, into a few nicks and scrapes. Two thorns of the crown had been broken off and lost. He carved thorns to replace them and glued his thorns in place, painting them with a very fine brush.

It was a long day's work, a grim day's work, and he felt when the day was over that he had filled the role of Joseph of Arimathea, or of whoever had worked for Joseph, in preparing the dead body of Jesus Christ for the tomb.

He walked out onto the busy streets of Munich, finding the acceptance of them difficult. Men and women were queuing up for streetcars, hurrying along the sidewalks, talking, gesturing, laughing. The Son of God had not died in Munich this day and the heavens had not opened and the graves had not given up their dead. It was merely Tuesday night.

There was only one other light besides his own in Streber Gardens, a light in a house far down the street. He did not know whose house it was because he did not know his neighbors. He and Ursula were ignored, denied acceptance in an odd country-town fashion, but they were not treated with hostility. There was hearty friendliness all around them on the weekends but they did not participate in it.

"Probably our own fault," he said. "We do not know how to make a place for ourselves."

He turned in at his own gate, happy to be home. The light in his windows, his and Ursula's, was a warm, pleasant light and he could smell the dinner when he opened the door. Ursula turned from the stove into his arms and he kissed her. Her eyes smiled up at him and this was how he had learned to anticipate his return home. There was someone waiting for him to arrive. Tonight, somehow, there was something missing, something that he could not define. It was, he thought, probably his own sense of guilt creating a barrier. It had been with him all day. Ursula waved toward the big boiler on the stove.

"*Suppe Ursula*," she said.

It was one of her achievements, a thick soup which she made out of assorted leftovers and a few added ingredients, meat or vegetable. She never seemed to know what was going into her soup, or what had gone into it; but she never had any doubt of how it would turn out. It amused him that she named it after herself. It was a trick that she had, a trick of possessing things, of drawing them to herself.

He went into the lavatory to wash. He could hear Ursula picking things up and laying them down. It was a good sound, a reassuring sound. He liked to know that she was there, in the house with him. His grim mood of the day was fading.

Her feeling for inanimate things, he thought, was oddly appealing. She identified so warmly with objects. A spoon that she used regularly became "my spoon" and the way in which she said that made the spoon an extension of herself. The linking of herself with objects was even more closely defined when it came to clothing. Pride lighted her voice when she spoke of a dress or a scarf that looked well on her or in which she looked well, and there was sympathy in her for something that had grown shabby. To a Monk who owned nothing of his own, who possessed all things in common or held them in trust, possession was a fascinating thing. Many people, he knew, expanded themselves outward into animals but he had never known anyone with Ursula's links to inanimate things, links of liking, of affection.

It was a strange meal. Ursula talked as she seldom did, a flow of words about little that mattered. Konrad's Monk soul, prizing the quiet and the contemplative and the utterance of that which was meaningful, shrank from the garrulity but he watched the girl's face with fascination. Her eyes seemed brighter than normal and she laughed at odd intervals, emphasizing or dramatizing some minor thought or incident beyond its true value. Her hands seemed almost at play on an instrument, moving with, or to, their own rhythm. They were eloquent hands, slender, with long fingers.

"I nearly forgot to tell you," she said suddenly in midnarrative, "your friend, the postman, was here, a man named Kurt Ziegler. He is the man who got this house for us. I did not know. He is very nice. He said that he will be back to see you. He has something to tell you."

Warning bells rang through the words. Ursula, of course, was unaware of them. "His brother is a policeman," Konrad said.

"Oh!"

"That has no significance. The brother, too, is a friendly man. His name is Bruno."

Konrad looked at his plate. He had eaten nearly all of his dinner. It had been a good dinner but the day had been a hell of a day. The message that Kurt Ziegler wanted to see him was not good news. It could only mean that their tenure of occupancy at Streber Gardens was drawing to a close. After that, what? He had never been able to formulate an answer in his mind although he had faced the problem many times mentally while engaged in some task which employed only his fingers. Streber Gardens was the dream existence, time borrowed from another person's life, the essence of the temporary and, in all of that, it lent itself perfectly to what he and Ursula were together, to what they had.

He heard the scrape of Ursula's chair and raised his eyes. She had pushed her chair back from the table and was sitting with her legs apart, outthrust, arrested in the pushing movement. She was staring at him and her expression was unreadable.

"I am a coward," she said. "I would rather go outside where it is dark. I will tell you here." Her lips trembled. "I got my letter back, Konrad. The postman brought my letter back. They do not know where Annchen is. There is no longer a school in Cihilka."

There was agony in her face, tears floating on the surface of her eyes. He crossed the small space, dropping on one knee beside her, gripping her hand with his.

"No matter," he said. "'Cihilka was a miserable place."

"But the children!"

"Are someplace else. You can do nothing about that."

"I know. I know." She slid off the chair, dropping to the floor beside him. She cried then, her head buried in his shoulder. He could feel her body shaking under his hand.

"I have nowhere to go, Konrad," she said, "nowhere to go."

He tried then, and through the dark hours of the night, to comfort her, to reassure her, to tell her that he had never wanted her to go back to Czechoslovakia, that he wanted her forever with him. She gripped him tightly, winding her body into his, kissing him fiercely then relaxing limply.

"It cannot be," she said. "You know that. It cannot be but I love you for wanting it to be."

"It will be," he said. "We will not go anywhere until we can go together."

He looked into the darkness where he so often saw things. There was nothing there, nothing at all. He did not have anything to give to Ursula and he was promising much, promising so very much. He tried to pray and the darkness mocked him.

Chapter Eleven

Konrad came home from a day of bronze angels to find Ludwig Rohne, Werner's father, waiting for him at the gate to Streber Gardens. The man's smile was broad under his bushy down-ended mustaches.

"A greeting to you," he said. "It has been too long. I would buy you a beer."

Konrad laughed. All that his shaky status in the neighborhood needed now was a night of drinking with Rohne, a vocal return, two men loudly singing.

"Unfortunately I do not seem to stop at one beer," he said.

"Neither do I. A man should not stop with one beer."

"All right. I will show you I shall stop with one."

Ludwig Rohne's eyes were laughing. "I do not bet."

They did not walk as far as they had walked before. There was a place with tables in a courtyard. The day was full spring. Some of the blossoms were gone but others had taken their places and there were tender leaves on the trees. Ludwig led the way to a table beside an old hooded well, used now mainly for pictorial effect.

"I have not seen Werner for a long time," Konrad said. "He has forgotten me."

"No. He speaks of you. He has little time." Ludwig slammed his stein against the tabletop. "By God, he is a good boy. You were right about the sketches. He has a talent, a good talent. There is a man, a scientist, who pays him to make sketches for a notebook. He is a poor man and he does not pay much, but the boy enjoys himself."

"I am certain that he does."

"*Ja*." Ludwig laughed. "I did not tell you. I made sketches once, too. It is hereditary with him. He gets it from me, that talent. In school I made them and in the army." He spread his hands apart. "The war took them. It took everything. No matter. It was a small talent."

"Do you believe that Werner's is a small talent, too?"

"Of course. What else? He is not Franz Hals, not anybody, just a boy who sketches. I told him this. I am proud of him. I do not expect anything of his talent but it is a family pride that he has it. He understands this."

Konrad drank his beer. It tasted well after a hard day and there was a mild anesthetic effect in it for the ache of unanswered questions. He did not know anything about relationships within a family, about who understood what, and why. He knew that there had been little understanding between Werner and his father only a short while ago.

"We are friends, my son and I," Ludwig said. "It is as I always wanted it to be. I understand his sketches. He came with me to the factory to see where I work."

"He did? What did he think of it?"

"He was astonished. He did not imagine so clean a place, so many fine machines. He was impressed with what I do. He did not imagine so many skills necessary, the responsibility."

Konrad looked into his stein. His beer was gone and he badly wanted another, but there was no point to it. A story had been told and he would succeed only in spending an evening beside this charming old well under a tree that was gently green. Werner, who had been in rebellion, had accepted an invitation to look with friendly eyes at the future which awaited him. Some day he would meet a girl. He would have a job in the razor-blade factory. He would have children who would be restless and dissatisfied but well-fed and well-clothed. Why not? How else could the world stay intact? He rose from his place.

"I am happy for Werner, and for you," he said. "I'm grateful for the beer. I must go now."

Ludwig Rohne looked astonished. "One never hears of such a thing. We have barely started. A single beer!"

"And good company. I could not ask for more."

He shook hands. He had called upon his willpower and he had walked away from the seductive comfort of beer and talk and a spring evening. Self-restraint was a simple exercise for a Monk but he had not restrained himself notably of late. It was good to know that he could still exercise a measure of self-control. In the midst of self-congratulation, he paused, breaking stride, hearing a voice from his long ago.

"When you are proud of a virtuous act, you have accepted payment for it," Father Stephen said. "You have sold the fruits of virtue cheaply. Pride! What can you do with that?"

One did not argue with Father Stephen nor with the memory of him. Konrad walked on slowly, thoughtful, humble in his vain glory.

Kurt Ziegler was sitting with Ursula on two of the kitchen chairs which were placed in the small cleared area in front of the house. Ziegler was wearing his post office uniform. He was smoking a cigarette.

"I still sit when I can," he said. "The lady happily offered chairs. She has also provided delightful company."

Ursula rose. "You were late. I will go back to my dinner. Mr. Ziegler is invited if he will stay."

"Couldn't possibly. Would enjoy it if I could." Kurt Ziegler's eyes followed Ursula when she went into the house. "There have been changes made if you do not mind my saying so," he said. "She was the world's most hostile woman when first I met her."

"She was ill. This house has been a good place for her, good for both of us."

"I am glad. I hoped that it would be." Kurt Ziegler looked embarrassed. He made a brushaway gesture with his right hand. "You have probably guessed why I am here."

"Yes. We will have to leave."

"That's right. I am sorry. The woman who owns the things in the house, certain rights to occupancy and all that, is coming back to settle affairs. She lives now in Stuttgart. I believe that I've told you that she was married to my wife's brother. Everybody here at Streber liked him. They like me and my brother Bruno."

"That is why they tolerated us, because they like you. They do not like us."

Kurt Ziegler's face was suddenly a mask. His eyes were intent. "You are difficult for them," he said. "You must understand that. You wore garments which they associate with the clergy. You proclaimed yourself a Monk. Yet, you have had a woman in the house with you all of this time. She is no longer ill."

He made the brushing gesture again when Konrad would have spoken. "Tell me nothing," he said. "I am not entitled to any explanations. I want none. I am merely explaining a situation to you. My sister-in-law of sorts will be in Munich three weeks from today. It would be better to go before she arrives. She can be a difficult woman."

"I will do that. You have been generous. I must owe you money."

"Not a cent. You cost me nothing. I am custodian of a kind for this place. You have taken good care of it for me. Enough. It does not, you understand, belong to anyone. It will, when paper work is completed, be available again to some worthy person of limited income."

"It is a remarkable idea."

"Yes." Kurt Ziegler rose and extended his hand. "I have enjoyed knowing you. I like the young lady. I hope that all goes well with you."

He was obviously a man easily embarrassed by situations. He turned abruptly, almost a military turn, and walked down the road. Konrad went slowly into the house. Ursula turned from the stove.

"That man, that postman," she said. "I remember only vaguely, not certain that I am remembering at all, when I first saw him. I asked you about him last night. He had something to do with our getting this place. He arranged for it."

"More than that. He had everything to do with our getting this place."

"Ah. Then now, his visit today, it means that we must leave?"

"Not immediately."

"How long?"

"Three weeks."

"Three weeks!" She repeated the two words as she turned back to the stove. Konrad was thinking that three weeks could be made to sound like a long interval of time but the time was actually short if one had a problem to solve, a problem such as his. Ursula's mind, obviously, had been balancing the same equation of time and things to do. She gave words to her thinking when they sat out of doors in the late twilight after dinner.

"Three weeks," she said. "What can we do in three weeks that we cannot do in one?"

"One never knows. One investigates possibilities."

"One does not do anything of the kind. There are no possibilities. You would do better, my Konrad, not to think of me. You have your work. You earn money. You are a man and welcome anywhere, or you are a Monk with even a wider choice. Your papers are all right. You can stay safely in Germany. Nothing hangs over you. Why should you take me on yourself, adding only problems that have no answers?"

"I love you."

"That is sweet. I am grateful. I shall remember that, but I am the only woman you have ever met. You do not know if another woman would be better for you."

"I want no other woman."

She laughed softly. "I believe you. But time passes. One forgets. I have nothing with which to hold you because I have nothing to offer you."

"You offer me everything."

"Me. Only me. I have nothing else. It would not be enough forever."

"Let me judge that."

"Yes. Of course. You will. You cannot see as far as I can see."

"I will find a way to marry you."

"Without papers? Without expelling me from Germany where I do not belong?"

He heard her voice and it faded out in the soft light. He was feeling as he felt during the nights of prayer when everything was right and good. The sense of presence was with him and he thrust out his hand toward Ursula, commanding her to be still. He rose and walked to the fence, feeling the sky press down. He did not see anything or hear anything. He had no awareness of time, no feeling that anyone existed in the world. Something held him, then let him go. He shook his head.

"Of course," he said.

He walked back to Ursula. She was staring at him, her eyes wide. "You looked so strange," she said.

"It makes no difference," he said. "We have been thinking all around our problem, not straight into it. Marriage is not words on a paper or records in a *Rathaus* or a blessing from a priest. Marriage is two people pledging themselves to each other before God."

He drew a deep breath. "When I went out with Father Stephen to the Catacomb Church people, there were some who had waited a long time for a priest to bless their marriages, but they were married because they wanted to be. I served Father Stephen at many, many church marriages but he always said that he did not marry these people; they married each other. He was only a witness. The Roman Church, too, maintains the same thing, as do other churches."

"What are you trying to say?"

"That we will be married. Everything else is subordinate to that. This will be our church, this house, because it is the only church we have. I know the ritual which asks God to bless us. We will marry each other."

She was still staring at him. "No," she said.

"Yes."

"No. You do not understand."

She rose abruptly and went into the house. He did not follow her immediately. He stood where he was, savoring the joy of feeling himself whole again, able to reach into a spiritual dimension, to move beyond the limitation of words, of all purely physical and material things. When he did go inside, Ursula was stretched across the bed, crying.

"What is the matter?"

He sat on the bed, resting his hand on her shoulder. She did not immediately answer but he could feel the vibration of her weeping through the thin fabric of her dress. He turned her body and lifted her onto his lap.

"Now, tell me," he said.

He had only a glimpse of her face before she hid it against his shoulder. She was a lovely woman. Her eyes were large, her nose short, her mouth wide and softly shaped, her skin satin smooth. She sobbed quietly for a minute then gripped him tightly.

"There is no one like you, Konrad," she said, "no one in all the world. I cannot marry you, not before God as you would have it, not any way that tied you to me."

"Why not?"

"I never wanted to tell you. The rape, Konrad. I hate now to speak of it. It injured something inside of me. I cannot have children but I can be a woman to a man. It is not enough for you. I am only half a woman, Konrad."

He held her, feeling shock. He had been a Monk, expecting no children, having no place for them in his life. He crossed a line and if he was to be a married man, he accepted the idea of a family, of children. The thought passed as it came. This was the woman sent to him by God. He had not sought a woman. If there were no children in God's purpose for him, he would accept that without questioning.

"You are all that I ask of God, Ursula," he said.

"You cannot feel like that. A woman owes you more."

"No. I do feel like that."

She clung to him and she cried again. This time he let
her cry without interrupting her, recognizing a necessity.
She refused to renew discussion of marriage but she was
stormily passionate and he felt that a decision had been
merely deferred. The timing was rightfully hers and he
left it to her.

She introduced the subject on Friday evening at an
awkward moment, an almost impossible time. Otto Genzelt
had come over to work on the garden for which Konrad
still lacked skills, a volunteer effort on Otto's part which
seemed to have meaning for him beyond his powers of
expression. Dinner was cooking on the stove and, outside,
the light was fading. Konrad went indoors for an al-
ternate hose nozzle, one that sprayed. Ursula gripped
his arm, turning him.

"Do you mean it, Konrad," she said, "that is, would
you want a marriage to me?"

"Of course. You know I meant it."

"Then I will."

He had a hose nozzle in his hand and he was aware
of Otto waiting outside. As a romantic moment this was
impossible. "I am glad," he said.

She seemed to be waiting for him to say more and the
words would not come. She shook her head. "You do not
sound glad."

She released him abruptly and went back to the cooking
of the dinner. He hesitated then let her go, making his
way outside to the waiting Otto. Some of the ease and
relaxation had gone out of his time with Otto because he
felt he had failed Ursula's moment but he could do nothing
about it. Otto, too, seemed to feel his unease and left
rather abruptly.

As though she realized that her timing had been at fault,
Ursula was brightly cheerful at the dinner table. She talked

about the neighbors who never spoke to her, telling him what manner of people they were, how they looked when they came in for the weekend with assorted bundles, loads, and packages for the time at Streber Gardens. He was helping her with the dishes when she returned to the subject of themselves.

"You are quite involved with that boy, Otto, aren't you?" she said.

"What do you mean by 'involved'?"

"You treat him like a son. And you aren't that old."

"I never thought of anything like that. He needs someone to like him, to share things with him."

"Why you?"

"There was no one else. I called on him when I needed help. He came through for me. Things happen, things work out. One does not analyze everything."

"He acts as though you were his father."

"He doesn't have a father."

"Well, he is an odd person, not at all likable."

There it was again. Otto would probably always face the grim fact that people were not attracted to him, that some people were repelled. "You don't know him," he said.

"Maybe not." She put a dish away then turned. "I cannot help feeling something about him. You were so eager to go back to him that the idea of marrying me was no longer important."

"It was important. You just picked the wrong moment. I want to marry you and you know it."

"Well, I won't pick the wrong moment again. I won't marry you."

"Don't then!"

The words came out explosively without his planning them. He was appalled but there was a swift angry current flowing through him. He tossed his dishtowel at the back of a chair and stalked out into the garden. He stood at the gate and there was sound along the road; voices, a musical instrument, the metallic semblance of a voice over a radio, laughter. There were lights, too, in all of the windows. He remembered another instance when he had thrown something down and stalked out.

It had been in Vienna during Father Stephen's last year when the priest was in bad health, beset by aches of various kinds and, at intervals, unreasonable. Konrad had stayed away for two hours on that occasion. When he returned, his anger had cooled and he tried to explain to Father Stephen why his temper had slipped out of control.

"It is unimportant, that," Father Stephen said. "I have forgotten what the difference was between us. I remember your action. You may very well have been right in the dispute but you lost my respect."

Father Stephen did not make his points as sharply, or as clearly, in those last years as he had made them once, but he made them. Now, in Streber Gardens, Munich, Konrad turned and walked back into the house. Ursula was sitting in the kitchen sewing a tear in a skirt.

"I am sorry," he said.

She lifted her eyes to his. "So am I. It was my fault. I kept thinking that you should not marry me, that you would want sons some day, not like Otto, better than Otto, your own."

"No."

Their eyes held, then she dropped the needle, the thread and the skirt. She was in his arms and he held her close. "Marry me," he said. "Tomorrow."

"No. I have no clothes. You have none."

"That is not important. There will be only the two of us here."

"It *is* important. I have saved more money than you can

imagine. They pay well, those nuns, and I spend carefully. You need clothes. Very desperately do you need clothes. We will shop tomorrow. I will buy a new dress. We will have to go to very reasonable places."

She was still planning the shopping trip after they had gone to bed. Konrad shrank from it but he recognized the area of decision as hers, looking forward in a premonitory sense to the realization that there would be other decisions that would also be hers, that he was no longer alone.

"We will be married on Sunday," he said.

Her voice came up to him, sleepily. "No," she said. "There will be so many people around on Sunday. Monday. Monday will be better. We will be alone. I want it quiet for my wedding."

Chapter Twelve

On the eve of his wedding, Konrad prayed for two hours and he insisted on returning for the night to his narrow cell-like room. Ursula, who had become involved in the idea of a wedding that must be taken as seriously as if there were a church filled with people, shook her head disapprovingly at the idea of the separation.

"There are a great many unrealities mixed in with your realities," she said.

As the evening shadows drew in on Monday, Konrad poured two cups of wine and lighted candles set in two ancient candlesticks. He had borrowed the candlesticks from the ancient Sister Agathe who had made him sign a receipt for them. Ursula had retired to the bedroom to dress. Konrad was wearing the suit that she had made him buy on Saturday. It was blue, a rough cloth, the first suit that he had ever owned and he was greatly impressed with it. Ursula had been less impressed.

"It will do," she said. "It is what we can afford. You will wear better some day."

He had a white shirt, too, and a plain blue tie with no pattern in it. Again, he had been guided by Ursula. "When

you can afford only a few things, it is best to have those
few things simple," she said.

Shoes were a problem that they could not meet. The
cost was too high. He owned heavy-soled hiking boots
which would not go well with the rest of his attire, and
he owned Monk sandals designed for indoors. Ursula con-
sented reluctantly to the sandals because there was no
alternative.

"I have nearly enough things myself," she said. "I will
not need much."

Even to Konrad's inexperienced eye, she was in need
of many things. Her clothes were those in which she had
worked as a governess. She had three pairs of shoes, one
pair of which looked very well when polished. She
bought a pair of stockings and a straight-line dress of navy
which she tried on three times before buying.

"You will have to marry me as I look," she said. "Some
day I will go to a beauty shop and you will not know me
when I come out. Not now."

"You are beautiful now."

"You are supposed to think so. I am not, of course."
She paused. "I would love to wear white but I no longer
have the privilege, do I?"

He frowned in concentration. "No."

Ursula laughed. "A wise woman would never have asked
a Monk such a question."

"I am no longer a Monk."

He knew that he was being stiff and literal, that he was
without humor, that Ursula was reaching desperately for
the light and the frivolous out of a mounting nervousness.
He could do nothing for her. He had to be both groom
and priest, calling upon God to bless the marriage in which
he was a partner. The calling upon God was, perhaps,
presumptuous. He was a man in sin, or, if God accepted

his intent to wed as an essential part of his union with Ursula, a man not in sin. One way or another, he had to call upon God and he was, at his best, a most unworthy creature.

As the time approached he placed two rings on the freshly laid tablecloth between the two lighted candles. He had made the rings in the afternoon from odd bits of silver in his repair kit. He would have preferred gold but he had none. On a chair in the background he had Father Stephen's crucifix and the small testament which was all that Stephen had been able to carry on the flight from Dresden.

He was ready. He walked to the door of the bedroom and knocked. Ursula came out and he did not know what she had done to herself but she was particularly lovely. He led her, on his left side, to the table and stood there with her. He had to leave his ghost self then beside her while he walked behind the table. He was remembering Father Stephen and those other weddings of the Catacomb Church, some of them almost as primitive as this. He did not have the great voice of Father Stephen but his voice, he knew, was good. He raised his eyes to the immensities beyond the low ceiling.

"God is the Lord," he sang in Church Slavic. "Bless the Lord, O my soul! O Lord, my God, Thou art very great. Marvelous are Thy works, O Lord. In wisdom hast thou made them all. Glory to Thee, O Lord, who has created all things."

Ursula's voice lifted. "Alleluia."

He had not been certain that she would remember. He had rehearsed her only once. He handed her one of the candles now and held one himself. They should be blessed but he had no power to bless anything, not even the humblest candle. They walked to the table and set the candles down, doing in two steps what should have been a solemn procession in the church.

"The servant of God, Konrad," he said, "is betrothed to the handmaid of God, Ursula."

The ceremony was as solemn now as a Mass. Silence surrounded them. The candles flickered slightly. They lifted the rings from the white cloth and presented them to each other, placing them on outthrust fingers. Lifting the candles they stepped away from the table, then back. They sipped wine from the cups three times. Konrad sang again in the ancient Russian of the Church.

"Blessed is everyone that feareth the Lord, that walketh in His ways.

"For thou shalt eat the labor of thine hands. Happy shalt thou be.

"The Lord shall bless thee out of Zion and thou shalt see the good of Jerusalem all the days of thy life."

Ursula remembered again, singing softly after each verse the phrase that he had taught her:

"Glory to Thee, our God, glory to Thee."

He lifted her hand then and said: "I take thee, Ursula, to be my wife for all the days of my life."

Her eyes were lifted to his and there were tears in them. "I take thee, Konrad, to be my husband for all the days I live."

He lifted his voice once more: "May we be blessed, O Lord, walking in peace and performing in righteousness the commandments Thou hast given us."

The ceremony was over. He felt that it had been inadequate, that he had not done the ritual well. He stood in the quiet room with Ursula beside him and there were great shadows on the wall. The candles were nearly burned out. He turned slowly and Ursula was in his arms. He kissed her and he had no words.

"Konrad," his wife said, "I will be faithful to you forever and I will share with you and risk with you and love you always. There is not, cannot be, in all the world another man like you."

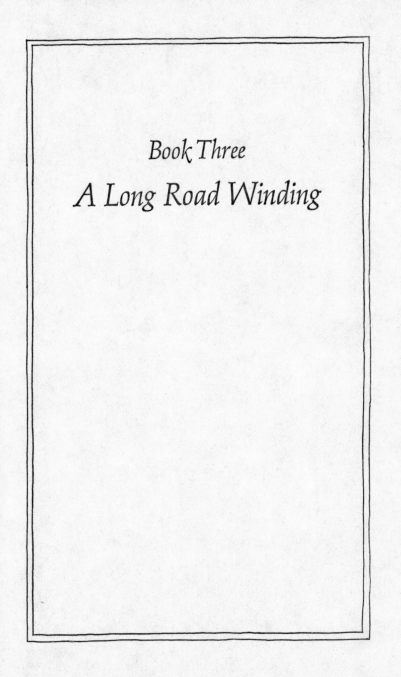

Book Three

A Long Road Winding

Chapter One

Three weeks was a languorous period of time as a honeymoon, a succession of days and nights of close companionship, of discovery, of adventure, of time drifting. Three weeks was hours racing into days and days turning as swiftly as leaves on a calendar when one measured them in terms of seeking solutions to problems. In three weeks one had to leave Streber Gardens and move to another shelter, somewhere.

Konrad had lived his life, or most of it, on shorter notice than three weeks. He had never needed so much as three hours to move out on the road. He had traveled much in Russia with Father Stephen and he had crossed Czechoslovakia with him after their escape from Dresden. All that either man possessed was wrapped easily into a small roll. He had traveled Austria himself, and Germany, working where he stopped, all of his tools, clothing, and small possessions in the cart that he pushed. He and Stephen had slept where they found shelter, in houses or barns or on the open earth. They were experts at improvising defenses against wind and rain and killing cold. They had stomachs adaptable to a wide range of food. Life as it came to one was something to accept and one wasted neither energy nor time complaining about it or wishing it other than it was.

"Happiness consists in learning to want less, not in forever striving to fulfill desires which only increase their demands on one, never diminishing them."

He could remember Father Stephen saying that. It had never been idle theory. Father Stephen had wanted little, needed little, and he was a happy man, sharing his happiness with others when he did not have a coin in his purse.

Konrad had learned to live with little and he had never developed any sense of possession. Nothing was his in any sense save the use made of it. A tool or a cart, necessary to him in the work from which he derived his living, was useful and he took care of it but he did not think in terms of owning objects. He worked and he sought work, not because he valued money but because he felt responsibility for himself. He had no claim upon the community in which he found himself for his daily bread.

Life had never been dull or lacking in anything that he really needed, if one ignored occasional hungry days or cold nights. There had been humor. Peasants never associated humor with religious people, and save for a rare few, never shared their humor with the religious; but Konrad could remember times alone with Stephen, in a barn or a cave or beside a campfire in open space, when they discussed incidents of their day and the grotesquely insincere solemnities of certain peasants who had tried to impress them, laughing uproariously.

Life had been crude, perhaps, but there had been color in it and vitality and reliance upon one's own skills. Vienna, of course, had softened the outlines of life and Stephen's illness had introduced needs that had not existed for them until then. They had still lived, however, the two of them, in the belief that they could justify existence only by what they brought into the world.

"Bring beauty," Father Stephen had said when Konrad was young. "If you can paint a picture or carve an image or plant a flower, you will have put something into the world that was not here when you came."

Later, he said: "When you repair something that has been broken, or restore something that has been injured, you have restored beauty to the world. That is good. Some people seem to live only to destroy, to bring ugliness to the place in which they live, to damage what they could not build. Avoid such people!"

They had been good, those days with Father Stephen. One could not bring them back out of memory save in small, odd pieces, but even the pieces were good.

All of that was changed now. Ursula could not live as he and Stephen had lived. Ursula needed many things and Ursula had to be protected from many things. He could not take to the road with her and not know where he was going, nor miss meals, nor sleep under the stars. The reality of a woman grew in a man's awareness; he did not see immediately the many strange ideas that were in her, the strong needs and wants, the odd necessities.

He went with Ursula on the streetcar to downtown Munich on a Saturday morning. He walked the busy streets with her and looked in the windows of shops. He had never paid attention to the items of apparel that women wore. It astonished him to see furs and fabrics and silks and taffetas through Ursula's eyes, to see earrings and pins and decorations to wear in one's hair. A woman's needs were endless, obviously, and he did not know at what point he could declare any item unnecessary in the face of Ursula's calm acceptance of the fact that the item was desirable. She had very little of the many things that she admired but the want of them was in her and the want seemed oddly reasonable.

They climbed Rubble Hill and he had a feeling of awe for what was beneath his feet. All those lives, all those symbols of lives! They looked down from the hill upon the excavation for the Olympic stadium, the wide field of Olympic construction. Off into the distance another line of excavation ran, Munich's subway in the making. The tall, thin saucer-tipped television tower threw a shadow on them but they did not go inside. They could not, they were certain, afford lunch in such an impressive place. They ate the small white sausages called *Weisswurst* at a roadside stand, washing them down with beer.

There were frivolous things such as the glockenspiel in the Town Hall, an open-air display of puppets in the tower; dancing, blowing trumpets, dueling in tournament fashion. Konrad watched the children in the crowd while watching the show.

"It must be wonderful to have something such as this in one's life when one is a child," he said.

"It is. Quite wonderful. You never had a childhood, did you?"

"Oh, yes. I had a childhood filled with remarkable experiences. I am glad that I had what I had, but there were no other children. I still marvel at city children. I do not know what they do. I do not understand their games."

"I will tell you sometime about the games they play," Ursula said.

She was, he thought, a child herself in many respects. He recognized in her many traits and mannerisms that had been latent in himself years ago, not permitted to develop. He was emotionally touched by some of her impulsive gestures, her capacity for excitement over trifles, unable to explain to himself why he should be stirred any more than he could explain his acceptance of desires in her that he would not countenance in himself.

In the evening they walked back to the streetcar hand in hand, feeling no self-consciousness. At Ursula's suggestion, they detoured slightly to walk on Promenadeplatz. They stood in the midstreet parkway and looked at the Hotel Bayerischer Hof.

Konrad remembered his journey to the hotel with Werner. He had been embarrassed at the necessity of entering the hotel and asking for Ursula's bags. He would be embarrassed tonight if he had a similar mission to perform. Ursula obviously had her own memories. She stood straight with her fists clenched.

"We are coming back here some day, Konrad," she said, "and we will have a room in that hotel and we will dine there and we will not be working for anyone."

The determination in her voice, the firm stating of a purpose, was frightening to Konrad. A person built future pain by wanting anything so intensely.

"It will not matter if we do not," he said gently.

She did not look at him. "It matters," she said, "and we shall do it."

They went to St. Ursula's Church on Sunday, not in time for the beginning of Mass but before the consecration. They had not planned attending the Mass, they were visitors to the church. Konrad had no feeling for the Roman Mass, no sense of reality in it and no prejudice against it. It could be, in Father Stephen's opinion, valid but it was probably heretical. That, to Konrad, was the enduring verdict. It interested him that Ursula, who proclaimed herself an unbeliever, genuflected before she entered a pew. She had been raised a Roman Catholic and she, too, had absorbed enduring verdicts.

They roamed the neighborhood afterward, driven to the

cover of doorways several times by sudden showers of rain. Ursula looked at the convent from the outside, the university buildings, the poor streets and the shabby streets and the streets on which proud people lived on little money.

"I like Munich," she said suddenly. "I did not believe that I ever would. We could stay in Munich, Konrad, when we move away from our house. We could find a place down here somewhere. It would have to be an apartment. Small. Not elegant. We could start as we must. You could keep your job."

He listened to her quietly. It was good for her to hope and to plan and to seek a pattern of life within which they could live, but he could not follow her hope to the point of faith. He did not believe that they could live in Munich.

There were many people in Streber Gardens who knew what they were and who they were. There were people in the neighborhood where he had first found Ursula, people who had been morbidly interested in the Monk who took a woman into his house. Any group of people anywhere expanded by a natural rule to many times its number. There were relatives and friends, people here and people there. Even in the world of monasteries, rumors and gossip and bits of information traveled with incredible speed; which Monks were becoming Soviet Monks, which ones were turning to the Catacomb faction, who was in favor, who in disgrace.

"If strangers, in a new neighborhood, accept me as your wife—and they would— Who is ever called upon to prove that she is married?—I could avoid any issue being made of papers," Ursula said. "I am a German married to a Russian who is also a German. I am very good with retarded children. I like to work with them. Not many people do. I could approach that work through a religious group, maybe one at that St. Ursula's Church, and no one would ask me for papers."

"You speak German with a Sudeten accent," he said.

"Would that make people suspicious?"

He smiled at the alarm in her face. "On the contrary. There are many Sudeten Germans, some with badly mixed-up papers. People are inclined to be sympathetic to them."

He could see Ursula being accepted as his wife without drawing questions or arousing suspicion if they were discreet, if they lived modestly and if he were employed; but the first doubt cast upon the fact that they were married would bring trouble crashing down upon them, demands for proof of identity and demands for proof of their marriage. They could not survive the first challenge and there were people in Munich, people whom he did not know, who might raise the issue.

"You can look at apartments," he said, "while I am at work and we will see what we can do."

Whether Ursula was right or not in her belief that they could live in Munich, he had no immediate alternative to offer. On the weekend he had no way of seeking alternatives.

Otto had been over on Saturday, working on his garden, and he had not even spoken to him. He had been away all day on the big trip downtown. Otto was over again on Sunday and he worked with him for a while in the afternoon then sat with him on a flat rock at the far end of the garden. The limb of a tree cast a shadow across Otto's face.

"You have done a lot of work on this patch of land," Konrad said.

"I liked doing it."

"That's the best reason for doing anything. Land knows when a person likes it."

"Do you believe that?"

"Yes."

"I do, too. Always did. I don't feel that way about people."

"People are more complicated than land, but people know, too, when you like them."

"Until I met you, I thought all people were sons of bitches. You know that."

"I am glad that you changed your mind."

"Maybe I didn't. I don't know."

"You've got to change it. People give you back what you give them."

"I don't know. You are the only one I ever met who did not think I was stupid because I wanted to drive a truck."

"It isn't stupid. A truck driver has to be a responsible man. He has to deliver goods safely. He has to drive well and not hurt anyone." Konrad spread his hands apart. "I have never known a truck driver but I would like to know one."

"So would I. I would like to travel, to see other places. Some people don't care, even Werner. Driving a truck I would see a lot of places. You really meant it, didn't you, when you said that I should do it."

"I do not say things that I do not mean."

Otto picked up a small pebble. He turned it in his hand, looking at it, then tossed it away. "That's why I like you," he said. "I've never liked anyone else except Werner."

It was growing dark. Ursula would be expecting him to come in. "We are going to have to leave this place," Konrad said.

"I know. That is why I wanted to talk to you. Where will you go?"

"I don't know. We looked at places near St. Ursula's Church. Do you know where that is?"

"Yes. It isn't far. I hope you get something there."

"We'll try." Konrad rose. "Do you have any suggestions?"

Otto shook his head. "That's another thing. Nobody but you would ask me for suggestions." He straightened his thin shoulders and lifted his head, looking toward the house. "I start my summer job again next week. I will drive the small truck for the Lagerhaus. I could help you when you move."

"I would like to have you help me." Konrad slapped the boy on the shoulder. "No one else will offer. We will do it together."

"Yes," Otto said.

He walked away and he did not look back. Konrad went slowly into the house. Ursula was setting the table. She looked at him sharply, then looked away.

"Dinner in five minutes," she said.

He would have liked to tell her about Otto. So much had been said that was not expressed in words. It might clear a few ideas but her dislike of Otto was a closed door. It would be impossible to discuss Otto with her. Closed doors between two minds made a conversation impossible. He talked at the dinner table about the St. Ursula neighborhood and that was a topic of lesser interest.

There was no time in his own week for exploring neighborhoods and he had no one to whom he could turn for suggestions, ideas, help. Ludwig Rohne was a hearty, friendly individual but it was impossible to imagine him as offering any suggestion of value. If Kurt Ziegler had had any idea of what they could do with the moving problem, he would have offered it when he brought them the news that his sister-in-law was returning from Stuttgart. Konrad remembered wryly that the postman had had the brilliant idea once of starting a rumor that Konrad and Ursula were brother and sister, escaping from the Russian government and meeting in Munich by prearranged accident. Nothing more had been heard of that story past its beginning. The hard-headed women of the community had obviously refused to accept it. Beyond those two men, Rohne and Ziegler, Konrad, as a solitary worker, knew no one.

Ursula, surprisingly, did nothing with the week as far as housing was concerned. She talked about seeking apartments but, after one afternoon of dubious effort, she waited until he would be able to accompany her. He did not know if she was timid about attempting something strange to her, afraid of strangers, or lacking in initiative.

A man could be married to a woman and know many things about her; yet discover in a situation without precedent that he knew nothing about her, that he could not predict what she would do.

He walked early to the bathhouse with Ursula on Saturday morning. Ursula went into the house when they returned and he stood by the fence, savoring the gently moving breeze, the perfume of blossoms, the voices of his neighbors along the road. It was a good morning and, in a short while, he and Ursula would go into the town and test the theory that it held a place in which they could live.

He saw the tall, heavy woman coming down the road, noting that she looked angry and combative. He was indifferent to her beyond the casual mental note. She stopped before his gate and there was something close to hatred in her face, a narrowing of her eyes, a twist of her mouth.

"You're the Monk, the one they call Konrad," she said.

"Yes."

"I'm Muriel Genzelt. You're influencing my boy. I want you to keep your dirty hands and your narrow Monk mind off him. I want you to leave him alone."

Her voice was loud and carrying. Other voices along the roadway were stilled. She was aware of those people along the roadway and she was talking for them. The flicker of her eyes indicated her awareness. She waved Konrad down with one outthrust hand when he would have answered her. She was, incongruously, wearing white gloves.

"I don't know what kind of a place you are running here," she said, "corrupting a boy's mind, leading him into rebellion against his own mother."

"He hasn't been corrupted. Not in any way."

Konrad heard Ursula open the door. She was behind him. The woman was aware of her, too.

"How can you say that he is not corrupted? You've been luring him down here where you and that bitch are living in sin, in vile, dirty sin, a disgrace to the fine place you are living in and an insult to the fine people that lived in it before you."

Ursula slipped past Konrad. She was a small, tense, compact person with clenched fists and with hot anger in her eyes. "Who are you calling a bitch?" she said.

"You."

The big woman spat at Ursula's feet. Konrad caught Ursula's arm when she would have swung her small fist. The woman at the gate could have broken her in two, and knew it.

"No," Konrad said. "It isn't worth it. She is what she is and you can't change that."

He felt Ursula trembling but he held her back. He was aware of the people in the road now. Nearly everyone in Streber Gardens had been drawn from their homes by the big woman's voice. She had an audience and she knew it, an audience friendly to her rather than to the people whom she accused. There was hatred in her. She pointed her finger, jabbing with it.

"You stay away from my boy," she said. "You let my boy alone."

She walked away, moving heavily. People cleared a path for her. Several of the women spoke to her and three women walked with her toward the gate. Konrad and Ursula stood together and nobody spoke to them. The crowd broke up into its separate units, two people or three, drifting away. Ursula's face was white.

"Her boy!" she said. "Who would bother with him? Look at her! That's his ancestry, his background . . ."

"His handicap," Konrad said.

Chapter Two

There was no point in house hunting or apartment hunting after Muriel Genzelt left. The plans for the day were canceled because Munich was canceled. One could not doubt that the noisy confrontation in Streber Gardens would be discussed by many people with many other people and there could be no doubt that the two persons accused by a boy's mother would be considered doubtful or unsavory characters. They were people who could not afford scandal or notoriety of any sort and there would be nowhere now in Munich where they could go and be safe from scandal and notoriety.

"Actually she accused us of nothing," Konrad said. "She implied, damnably implied, so many things. She told me to keep my dirty hands off him and she mentioned corrupting a boy's mind and she spoke of luring him. Nobody handled him, nobody corrupted him, nobody lured him."

"You should have let me hit her."

"It would only have involved you in more trouble."

"She called me a bitch. That was more than an implication."

Ursula's mood was stormy, then she was gone. She went into the bedroom and Konrad let her alone. There was nothing that he could do for her, nothing that he could say. They had less than a week left in Streber Gardens, if they were not asked to leave sooner, and they had no place to go.

Otto came a little after sunset. He walked in with more assurance than Konrad had ever seen in him. He seemed to be standing straighter, too.

"I was working all day," he said. "I heard about it just now. I didn't know that my mother was coming here."

"I know you didn't."

"I told her that I am through with her if she does another thing like that. I'll move out. I could. She doesn't believe it but she is afraid of it. I could. I will."

"It's all right, Otto. Not your fault. We were going to have to leave anyway. You know that."

"I know."

Otto looked away. He seemed to slump out of the erect, angry pose that he had maintained until now. Konrad tried to imagine him standing up to that big, coarse, rough woman, not doubting that he had done so.

"Anyway," Otto said, "I'm sorry about it. I'll help you move. You could leave a message for me at the Lagerhaus."

"I will."

Konrad watched him walk down the road. In this instance, Otto had been more articulate than he. There were times when words did not serve a man, when words would not come.

He went in the house and the bedroom door was closed. Ursula wanted to be alone and he could understand that. He sat on the ground that, in a sense, had become his ground for a short interval of time. He rested his back against the wall of the house. This was the place where he prayed but there was no prayer in him. He could understand that, too. Prayer in this moment would be a seeking for aid. He had done enough of that.

"All that you do, and all that you learn, prepares you for that which some day you must face," Father Stephen said.

The remark had been cryptic in its time, without meaning for him. It had meaning now. He had done many things, learned many things, but he had never seemed prepared for the things that he faced. When Ursula was a strange girl in the street, an alleged Russian, he said that he would take care of her and nurse her back to health, but he could not have moved her without Otto and the amazingly available truck. He had had no facilities for nursing and caring in that bare American building and the police would not let him stay there with a woman. He had no answers of his own but that stranger, Kurt Ziegler, had obtained this place for him.

He had no answers now but he could no longer rely on help from outside himself; the answer was somewhere within him and he had to find it.

Ursula was fixing their dinner when he went into the house. If she had been crying, she showed no evidence of it. He lifted her chin with one finger and kissed her. "We are going to be all right," he said.

"I know. What are we going to do?"

"I'll tell you after dinner."

They walked away from Streber Gardens. Some instinct took them to the clearing and the small American building. It looked shabbier to Konrad's eyes than the building he remembered but nobody had vandalized it. He had stopped what was probably the only attempt. Germans, young or old, were not by nature vandalizers. They liked to build, restore, re-create in kind.

Ursula shook her shoulders and walked away from the

clearing. "I don't know why I came back," she said. "I do not want to remember." She paused. "And I do not want you to remember."

"I have forgotten already."

Remembering or forgetting, they were very close in companionship on the road back; not hand in hand but touching occasionally, aware of each other.

"It is after dinner," Ursula said, "and you have not told me what we are going to do."

"We are going to move, of course. It cannot be Munich. We will have to go to another German city."

"Which one?"

"I cannot tell you yet. I will know next week."

"You better know next week. That is when we have to move."

It was characteristic of Ursula that she did not pin him to specifics. She either suspected that he did not yet know what he would do or she was willing to wait on his timing. On Sunday she was in a talkative mood. The neighbors ignored them more pointedly than they normally did so they stayed in their own garden with the flowers.

"I expected a committee or a delegation of neighbors telling us that we are undesirable," Konrad said.

"I didn't. They know that the woman is coming back, the postman's sister-in-law. They can hardly wait, I'll bet, for her to throw us out bodily, perhaps with the police."

"We won't wait."

"Wherever we go, whatever city, we will have to live differently," Ursula said. "I need my work, too, some chance to do what I can do. You understand, don't you?"

"Yes. I do."

"It has to be a fairly big city, or a very big one, so there will be schools for retarded children, somebody interested in them and working with them."

"Yes."

"We will have to have a radio."

"Why?"

"We never know what is happening. We do not know anything. We had a radio in the school at Cihilka. I listen sometimes here when I go to the store. We should take a daily newspaper, too."

"Why?"

"All the same reasons. The way we live, we do not know anything about the world in which we live, or what is happening."

"Could we change anything if we knew?"

"That isn't the point. We don't have to change anything, but we do have to be a part of the world we live in. We should know what people are doing."

He thought about Ursula's idea on the long walk to work on Monday morning. It was, he assumed, blind of him that he did not agree with her, could feel no interest in news or affairs beyond his own sphere of observation and activity. He enjoyed reading an occasional newspaper when one came his way, but he had never established understanding of newspaper sequence, of the stories today which were linked to previous stories, of long strings of event and circumstance continuing and being written about seriously each day. His blindness, if that is what it was, existed from his beginnings in the monastery. He had studied many subjects, some of them profound, but he had no history save that of the Church. Without links to contemporary history or a foundation erected on the history of the past, Church history was vaporous, of little interest.

If Ursula wanted a radio and newspapers, he supposed that they would have them as soon as they could afford them; but he would not learn easily to regard them as essential to his life.

As soon as he reached the convent he sent word to the Mother Superior that he would like to see her. She saw him at 10:45. She was seated behind her desk and there was no light in her features, no warmth in her eyes. She waited for him to speak without even a greeting or a good morning.

"I cannot work here any longer," he said. "This is my last week. I wanted you to know."

"You surprise me. I thought that you were happy with the work that we provided for you. Where has it failed you?"

"Nowhere. I have been happy with the work. I have to leave Munich. Personal reasons."

"You will go where?"

"I do not know. I have to ask your advice."

"Advice is easy to give and worth little. I would have to know more about your reasons for leaving us and more about what you want."

"I am married," he said. "My wife's identification is Czechoslovakian. If challenged it will not stand up. It is likely to be challenged in Munich."

"Married." The Mother Superior looked doubtful. "Your predecessor had a weakness for alcohol. He was not a Monk. Why would another city be easier on improper papers?"

"We would be unknown. If I had a job and my wife had an opportunity to do her work, with people taking her for granted, we might live simply without anyone challenging us."

"You might. You might not. You say 'her work.' What is her work?"

"Teaching retarded children. She has a genius for it."

The Mother Superior moved slightly. "Interesting. Interesting indeed. You want something from me? Precisely what?"

"I would like to do what I do here in another city, a city with a school for retarded children. I would work in a convent or a museum."

"I have little to do with museums. I do have communication with convents. Many of them restore art objects, as we do, or as we try to do; not their own, work brought to them."

"Where would you suggest that I go?"

"Stuttgart or Frankfurt."

"I would take Frankfurt if I have a choice."

The Mother Superior frowned slightly. Emotion on her face was a rare thing. The frown came swiftly and vanished as it came.

"I would have suggested Stuttgart," she said. "Frankfurt is a dull and ugly place. It was ruined in the war and it is depressingly modern. No matter. You are a good man at your craft. I will write a letter of inquiry to Frankfurt."

"Thank you." Konrad hesitated. "If I paid the toll charge, would you phone instead of writing?"

There was a moment of silence. The Mother Superior made a gesture of dismissal. "I will phone. I will send for you if I have any news."

Konrad went back to his workroom. He was surprised to discover that he was covered with sweat, that his shirt stuck to his skin. "I wrong that woman every time that I so much as think of her," he said. "She is a fine person and I do not like her."

Chapter Three

"There must be something wrong with us," Ursula said. "People who are leaving a place forever should say good-bye to somebody."

Konrad shook his head. He had never lived in a world where good-byes were said. A Monk packed the few things that he needed and left one place for another. Other Monks discussed him for a short time or told anecdotes about him but if he did not return he became a thin figure, forgotten by most of those who had lived with him and served with him. Konrad had found Munich similar to the monastery. If he had touched lives, he had touched them lightly. He could remember faces, pleasant experiences, friendly exchanges; but he did not belong in any of the lives and none of the remembered people belonged in his life.

Werner? Yes. He had felt close to Werner for a time and he had liked Werner's father. Neither of them needed anything that he had, anything that he could do.

"We will have to live differently wherever we go," Ursula said. "People should have friends, people with whom they share things."

"And a radio and newspapers."

"Yes. A radio and newspapers and friends. Those are normal things. Without them, we are not normal people."

Konrad laughed softly. It always amused him when Ursula became solemn and serious about anything, but he found her disturbing, too, when she was in a serious mood. She was changing his life and she would probably change it more radically in the months and the years ahead. She always had a certain logic on her side, a logic that he respected even as he resisted.

On Wednesday morning at 9:30 the Mother Superior sent for him. She had a small pile of papers on her desk. "There is a convent in Frankfurt," she said. "It is larger than this and the custodian for many damaged objects, some of which are of great age. They have needed a man of such skills as yours and I have recommended you highly."

"Thank you. I am grateful."

"Do not be. I have given you only what you have earned. My recommendation covered only your work and your record of dependability here. I gave you no moral endorsements. I know nothing of your personal life, habits, or disciplines."

Konrad could think of no comment and, obviously, none was expected. The Mother Superior lifted another sheet of paper. "Here is the name of the convent, its address, and a note to Mother Gertrud. She will pay you a larger salary than I did. I have written, too, the name of a priest who is dedicated to retarded children. He may work minor magic with papers or work permits, whatever is necessary."

It was more than a man had the right to expect. Konrad swallowed hard. "I have enjoyed working for you," he said, "and I will miss this place."

"No one here works for me. You worked for God. He will be good to you in Frankfurt, I hope. Good-bye."

She extended her hand and he took it in his, surprised at how small it was. There was still no warmth in her eyes, no expression in her face that he could read; but he knew that he would remember her, one of the few people whom he would remember.

There were horse chestnut trees in bloom along his route home, the green limbs decorated with the proud white blossoms that looked like candles. He was feeling slightly dazed, a dweller in unreality. He remembered Ursula standing at the gate with him last night. They had found it impossible to sleep and they had gone out to the quiet and the peace of Streber Gardens at 2 A.M. There did not seem to be another person on earth but themselves.

"The chestnuts are blossoming," Ursula said. "In Kladno, where I grew up, the storks came when the chestnuts lighted their candles. They built nests in the housetops."

Konrad had seen the storks, too, in Russia, and during his term as a farmer in Czechoslovakia. "I remember storks," he said, "because stork is one of the few bird names that I know. All the others are merely yellow birds or blue or red . . ."

He remembered now, walking home for the last time to Streber Gardens. He and Ursula had built memories together. He did not build them with anyone else.

She did not expect him so early in the day but she knew that the suspense was over when she saw his face. "Where?" she said.

"Frankfurt."

"It's the one you wanted. That nun liked Stuttgart better."

"Maybe we would. The woman who owns the things

in this house, Kurt Ziegler's sister-in-law, lives in Stutt-gart. It is a big city, but . . ."

"Oh, I forgot. We couldn't risk her. How did I forget? Never mind. Tell me all about it."

He told her all about it and he opened his last envelope to discover two extra days pay. He sat for a long time looking at the money before he put it away.

"That wraps it up," he said. "We're packed. If Otto can help us, we will leave this afternoon."

"We could manage without him."

"No."

He walked down to the Lagerhaus and Otto was open-ing a crate of farm equipment, a machine that Konrad did not recognize. He straightened when he saw Konrad and his lips tightened.

"You got word," he said.

"Yes."

"Where?"

"Frankfurt."

"When?"

"Today. This afternoon if you can help."

"I can help."

"I'll pay for the truck. We'll need it."

"You don't have to pay."

"I can. I have enough."

"It's something I can do. I'm doing it."

Otto turned away. He walked the length of the big room and entered the office in the rear. He came back within five minutes. "We'll go now," he said.

"Fine."

Konrad rode beside him and Otto steered the truck out of the Lagerhaus yard. This, Konrad thought, was in miniature what Otto wanted to do. Some men had an understanding of machinery, a feeling for it, a pride in what machines, properly handled, could do.

"You'll drive that big truck some day, Otto," he said.

"I'll try. It won't be soon. I won't see you when you go to Frankfurt."

"Maybe I'll spend my life there. You will visit me in the big truck."

"I'll want your address."

"When I have one, I'll send it."

Words did not come easy. There was so little to say. The truck stopped at the Streber Gardens gate. Ursula was standing outside the house. "I am trying not to cry," she said. "Isn't that stupid?"

"Yes."

Konrad walked past her. All of their things were packed. He had voted twice against taking his cart which he would never push on the road again, and he had vetoed his own rejection. The cart was packed and was going with them. It could be fitted into the train compartment as easily as luggage. The luggage, of course, was Ursula's. Werner had helped him to bring it away from the Bayerischer Hof. He looked around the kitchen, then crossed to the bedroom door and stood, looking in. Ursula came up behind him and put her arms around him.

"We'll be all right," she said. "Frankfurt will be a happy place for us."

He pressed her fingers. "Yes," he said.

Otto came in and helped him carry out the things that they owned. It was a long ride to the station, a silent ride. No one seemed to feel like talking. There were train tickets to buy and luggage to be hauled again. Otto stood on the platform outside their compartment window. He had said something but Konrad did not know what he said. It was not good-bye. The train started to move and the boy stood there. He did not raise his hand or make a gesture. Ursula's hand rested on Konrad's.

"It isn't good for a boy to have a Father Stephen too long," she said softly. "He has to learn to be himself."

Konrad turned his head. He could no longer see the figure on the platform. "I don't know," he said. "I am not certain."